ONLY US

Written by:

Shani Greene-Dowdell

This is a work of fiction. Names, characters, businesses, places, events, and incidents are either the products of the author's imagination or used fictitiously. Any resemblance to actual persons, living or dead, or actual events is purely coincidental.

Only Us
Published by Shani Greene-Dowdell Books
www.shanigreenedowdell.com
Cover design by ibdesignz
Edited by Shani Dowdell
ISBN: 9798287193539 | Independently Published
First Edition: 2025
For more books by Shani Greene-Dowdell, visit www.shanigreenedowdell.com or follow on social media.

Hey LoveBug,

First off, thank you. 📷

Whether you've been rockin' with me from the very beginning or you're just now pulling up to the party, I'm so glad you're here.

What you're about to read is a *Only Us*—a love story that's messy, grown, and from the heart. It's about betting on yourself, finding real love after heartbreak, and learning that the right person will *always* show up for you. Every time.

To my day-one readers: thank you for being with me through every plot twist, steamy moment, and "Oh no he didn't!" scene. You keep me going.

To my new readers: welcome lovebug. Get comfy. This is a safe space for anyone who loves a good story, believes in love, and doesn't mind a little drama and steam with their tea. 🍵

Now go ahead and dive in.

Meet Maya and David. Their story starts with a goodbye, but trust me, where it ends? Whew.

Love always,

Shani 💜

"Sometimes you have to lose it all to gain everything."

Table of Contents

Hey LoveBug, ... 3

Chapter One 7

Maya 7

Losing It All 7

Chapter Two 15

David 15

Almost Had it All 15

Chapter Three... 29

Maya 29

Time Changes Things 29

David 47

Little Firecracker 47

Chapter Five 65

Maya 65

Call Him Chaos 65

Chapter Six.. 77

David 77

Loving You Was Complicated....................................... 77

Chapter Seven 99

Maya 99

Miss Proactive Firecracker 99

Chapter Eight 113

David 113

Playing Games.. 113

Chapter Nine 123

Maya 123

The Governor's Ball 123

Chapter Ten... 141

David 141

What is She Doing? 141

Chapter Eleven 151

Maya 151

This is Crazy 151

Chapter Twelve.. 159

David 159

Not Yours Anymore 159

Chapter Thirteen 169

Maya 169

Oh, I Think I Like Him 169

Chapter Fourteen 183

David 183

Betrayal on Betrayal.. 183

Epilogue... 203

David 203

One Month Later 203

Amiri and Tess's Wedding Day 203

Chapter One

Maya

Losing It All

"Trinkets and lace? That's what the fuck this is all about?"

Troy's words hit the air with enough fire to burn me. I flinch at the anger in his tone. He didn't used to talk to me like this, but right now, he's standing at the door of the apartment we used to share with his arms crossed, looking like he's two seconds away from losing his mind. I've seen this look before. It's the one he used to wear when we had disagreements, but this time, what we are going through feels so big. It feels final.

Noticing Troy hasn't taken off his jacket, like he's not planning to stay long, I set the packing tape down on the half-empty box in front of me and stare at him. My fingers twitch with the urge to throw the tape at his head.

"You know damn well it's not about trinkets, Troy!" I say, my voice on edge. "It's about me. My dream. You knew this was something I've wanted for years."

He laughs, the taunting sound ricocheting around the nearly empty room, feeling like a slap to my jaw. "No, I didn't know about this for years. I have no recollection of you ever talking about leaving a six-figure career to play dress-up in a boutique."

My breath catches in my throat, and for a second, I don't even know what to say. If he thinks I'm quitting my job to play dress up, what could I possibly say to him? I grab the edge of the couch to stop myself from falling over his words. "Wow, Troy. That's... wow," I manage, blinking at him. "So, what I want, what I've been working toward, it's just some childish fantasy to you?"

Troy throws his hands up and looks at me like I have screws loose in my head. "Maya, come on. You had it made! You had stability, benefits, a retirement plan. You were set! Now you're tossing it all away to go play dress peddler in country-ass Azalea Cove?"

"Dress peddler?" My voice falls into my throat, and I'm surprised I'm even able to get the words out with how offended I am. "I'm opening a boutique. A bridal boutique. Do you know how many people dream of building something from the ground up? Of seeing their name on a business? Of creating something that's theirs? But sure, let's call it 'playing dress peddler.'"

He exhales loudly, pinching the bridge of his nose like I'm tap-dancing on his last good nerve. "It's not about dreams, Maya. It's about being realistic. You're leaving behind a corporate career in marketing that many people would kill for. You're trading that for some... some boutique in the middle of nowhere."

"Azalea Cove isn't the middle of nowhere," I snap, missing the point on purpose. "And it's not some boutique. It's *my* boutique. If I can market products for someone else, I can market my own!"

His jaw tightens, and his voice lowers in a way that used to make me stop and listen, but not this time. Not today. "And what happens when this plan you and some random women you met at a wedding expo fails? What happens then, smart-ass Maya?"

There it is. The thing I'd been waiting for him to say. The fear he's been trying to mask under all this "realistic" talk that caused him to move out of our apartment while he 'sorts things out in his mind.'

I shrug, trying to brush his words off as if they didn't just knock the wind out of my chest. "I'm not going to fail. And if by some small chance I do, then I'll rebuild. Or figure something else out. But at least I'll know I tried. I won't be sitting in an office ten years from now, miserable, wondering what could've been."

He shakes his head and steps closer. His eyes search mine like he's still trying to find the old Maya, the one who always played it safe. "Maya, listen, this isn't you. You're smarter than this. You're better than this. Don't do this to yourself."

I laugh, but he hasn't said anything funny. "I'm not doing anything to myself, Troy. You already made your decision. You left. You walked out on me because you didn't agree with my choice. So, don't come back here now, trying to talk me out of it like you're doing me a favor. You made it clear where you stand."

He shifts uncomfortably, his hand brushing over the back of his neck. "I just... I didn't think you'd actually go through with it. I thought after I gave you some space you'd come to your senses."

"Well, I didn't change my mind." My voice hardens as I fold another box shut. "And I'm actually fully aware of what I'm doing. So, if you came here to talk me out of opening the boutique, you're wasting your time."

He glares at me for a moment before he shakes his head and turns toward the door. "Fine. Do what you want. But don't say I didn't warn you."

"Oh, don't worry. I don't plan to say anything to you after today." I follow him to the door, not because I want to see him leave, but because I need to see him leave. I need to see him walk away from me again, so I'll know it's real.

He pauses in the doorway, one hand on the frame as if he's about to say something else, but he doesn't. Instead, he just looks at me long enough to make me second-guess everything before finally stepping out and closing the door behind him.

The click of the lock feels louder than it should. I stand there for a moment, staring at the door like it's going to swing open again. Like he's going to come walking back through the door and declare his love, support, and care for me. But it doesn't open again. The door to our relationship is closed. He's gone, just like he said he would be.

I turn around and absorb the room; the half-packed boxes, the empty shelves, the lingering smell of the cologne he left behind. The room is too quiet, the kind of quiet that feels like it's choking the life out of you. This is the moment everything hits me. It's over. Troy is really gone. The man I thought was my partner, the one I thought would stick by me no matter what, has decided that my dream isn't worth the risk. That I'm not worth the risk.

For a moment, I let myself feel everything. The hurt and disbelief smack me in the tear ducts, making me cry like a baby. I'm so confused. I have so many questions that are left unanswered. How could he love me but not believe in me? How did I not see this coming with Troy—a man I thought I would love forever?

My chest tightens as I replay his words in my head, the ones that cut the deepest. *"What happens when it fails?"* It's like he was rooting for me to fall flat on my face. And the worst part? He didn't even care enough to stay and see what would happen.

I stare at the half-packed boxes around me, my hands curling into fists at my sides. How dare he? How dare he walk out on me like this? Like I'm some impulsive fool chasing a pipe dream. The hurt and disbelief twist into anger and I can feel it rising in my chest. This was the man I thought I'd spend my life with, the one who'd promised to have my back no matter what. And now he's gone, just like a ghost, making me wonder if any of it was ever real.

I grab a photo frame from the table, one of the two of us on vacation. Back then the world was ours. We were so in love, so inseparable. That was then. This is now.

Without a second thought, I hurl the photo across the room. The glass shatters against the wall, the sound piercing and satisfying. It feels good to destroy something about us that used to mean the world to me, but it's not enough. I also want to scream, to cry, to do something that matches the way I feel. Instead, I sink onto the couch, my head in my hands.

Minutes pass, or maybe just seconds. I don't know. Eventually, the anger dulls down enough to quiet my spirit. Slowly, I stand, wiping at the corner of my eye before it betrays me with tears. I grab the tape again and seal another box, each pull of the tape feeling like a step forward, a move toward a future that's mine. Only mine.

If there's one thing I know for sure, it's this: I can't rely on anyone else to believe in me. Not Troy, not anyone. My family has given me their support, but if this dream is going to come true, it's going to be because I made it happen. And that's all I need. Just me.

I glance around, my eyes landing on the boxes stacked neatly in the corner. Each one is a reminder of the life I'm leaving behind; of the ten years I spent building a career that was never really mine. For two years, I thought Troy was my rock, my person, the one that would forever have my back. And now, he's gone.

My eyes land on another photo of us on the wall. We're smiling, arms wrapped around each other, looking like one of those picture-perfect couples in a magazine. I take it down. My fingers tighten around the frame, and without thinking, I throw it into the trash bag beside the couch. My breath hitches as the glass shatters, but it feels... freeing. Like I'm finally letting go of something I've been holding onto for too long.

I grab my laptop off the coffee table and place it in its bag. This device holds details of every expense, every projection, and every goal for the boutique. My boutique. Troy doesn't believe in me. Fine. I believe in me. And that's enough.

I sweep up all of the glass and remnants of the pictures, put them in the trash bag and tie up the bag filled with the photo and any other reminders of Troy. I set the bag by the door and take a deep breath.

This is it.

The end of one chapter and the beginning of another.

Chapter Two

David

Almost Had it All

It's been a hell of a day.

Six hours of back-to-back study groups, a mock trial that went completely sideways, and a professor who seems hell-bent on making sure no one walks into the bar exam with confidence. My brain feels like it's been stuffed through a meat grinder, and I'm running off legal briefs, vending machine snacks, and the fear of failure.

But none of that matters now.

I kept telling myself all day *just get through this, and I'll get to go home to see my baby.*

Every single day, getting back home to her is my prize. She's my peace and my future.

We're not in the same classes, but Danielle is usually at the study sessions with me, scribbling down

15

notes like her life depends on it. But lately, she's been pulling away, skipping sessions, and saying she needs to focus on her art. She says it calms her and gives her space to think.

If I had her talent, I'd dive into painting too, especially when the pressure builds. I also know how badly she wants to be a lawyer. Studying is important. Staying locked in matters. So, I plan to have an important conversation with her tonight about her future.

Not to mention, I miss her. Not just her sitting next to me in the study sessions, but I miss the way our iron sharpened each other's. Our late-night debates, the flashcard drills between kisses and making love, were everything. She's the reason I made it through every semester of college. The reason I can say I ever fell in love. The thought of walking across that stage and not seeing her beside me... I don't even want to think about it.

Even today, during a group session, when Raquel from Torts slid closer than necessary and kept brushing her knee against mine, I didn't even flinch. Didn't even entertain it. All I could think about was Danielle. About getting home to her. About the way her lips part just a little when she's focused. About the way she pushes me to do better. About the way she always steals fries from my plate, swearing she doesn't want her own.

So, I picked up her favorite Thai food with extra peanut sauce, no cilantro and stopped by the corner shop for peonies. She always says they make the whole apartment smell like sunshine.

With all of my treats in hand, I finally make it home. I push the door open with my elbow, a brown bag of takeout in one hand and a small bouquet of flowers in the other. The first thing I notice is that the lights are dim. Too dim. I don't feel the electric vibe I usually feel when I walk into our apartment. The space feels still. It feels abandoned.

"Danielle?" I call out, kicking the door shut behind me.

When I get no answer, I wonder if she's painting with her headphones in again. I grin to myself, already picturing her sitting cross-legged in one of my hoodies, splattered in paint, lost in her world.

But the silence is too still.

There's no soft music, no trail of sandalwood and vanilla she usually wears. Just... quiet. And that's when something in the kitchen jumps out at me. It's a single sheet of paper on the counter with my name written at the top in her handwriting.

She left a note?

I freeze mid-step. She's always home, never goes anywhere alone. Even when she goes to her parents', she wants me to go with her.

I set the food and flowers down and slowly pick up the letter.

David,

I'm sorry, but I can't do this anymore.

Please don't try to find me.

I need something different.

Forgive me.

—D.

A mixture of confusion and shock rule my thoughts. My chest feels like it's cracking open, like someone took a sledgehammer to my ribs. The letter trembles in my hand before falling to the nearest stool. I forget how to breathe. My woman is gone, and all I have is a note telling me not to try to find her as if I would give up on her so easily. I could never do that.

She knows I wouldn't do that.

Something isn't right.

Danielle *never* goes anywhere without telling me. She hates being alone, always rides shotgun even for late-night gas runs, and clings to her routines like gospel. I look at the note again, like maybe it'll offer some kind of clue as to what really happened to my woman, but the words stare back at me with cruel clarity.

"David, I'm sorry, but I can't do this anymore. Please don't try to find me..."

I take out my phone and immediately start calling her. A letter won't do. I need to hear those words in her voice. I need to know that she is okay and this is really what she wants. I need to talk to my baby to find out what happened to make her feel this way.

There's no answer, so I text.

I call again.

And again.

And again and again.

Still nothing.

My thumb hovers over the screen, hesitation creeping in. I don't want to call her mother and worry her with this. I really don't, but I'm running out of options.

I scroll through my contacts and find her mom's number. Mrs. Harper has always been kind to me. She was almost like a second mother during our undergrad years. She used to send us care packages and ask me if I was keeping Danielle focused on her studies.

My thumb taps the call button before I can talk myself out of it.

It rings twice.

"Hello?" Her voice is soft, warm, like always.

I swallow hard, trying to keep my tone steady. "Hey, Mrs. Harper. It's David."

"David!" she says, surprised. "It's been a while, honey. Everything alright?"

My throat tightens. I can't drop this on her. Can't tell her about the note, the silence, the fact that her daughter vanished like smoke in the middle of the day. She doesn't need that kind of worry unless I know for sure something's wrong.

"Yeah," I lie, the word causing me physical pain in the chest. "I was just trying to get in touch with Danielle. She's not answering her phone."

"Oh..." There's a pause on her end. "I haven't heard from her in a couple days. But that's not unusual, you know how she is when she's in her study mode."

"Right," I say, trying to make my voice sound casual. "I just thought maybe she'd mentioned something to you. Plans, travel, or anything like that?"

"Not to me," she replies, concerned now. "Is everything okay? You don't know where she is?"

I force out a chuckle. "She wasn't home when I came in from class this evening, but I'm sure it's fine. She probably just needed a little space to clear her head."

"Well, if I hear from her, I'll tell her you're trying to reach her."

"Thanks, Mrs. Harper. Appreciate you."

We say our goodbyes, and I hang up. My hand drops to my lap, the phone still warm against my palm.

I sit there for a second, staring at nothing. That knot in my gut pulls tighter.

Then I dial again. This time, it's a call to Danielle's best friend, Rolisha.

Straight to voicemail.

"Come on, Ro. Pick up," I mutter, rubbing my hand over my face.

I hang up and call again.

Again, there's no answer.

I drop my phone on the couch beside me, jaw clenched.

The silence is louder than ever.

It's starting to sound like a warning.

The room starts spinning as panic grabs me in a chokehold. I pace the apartment like a caged animal, staring at her things. Her sketchbook is open on the coffee table, her shoes are still neatly by the door, and her favorite hoodie draped over the back of the chair like she just stepped out to grab the mail.

If she was leaving, why would she leave everything behind?

Something's wrong.

My mind spirals into worst-case scenarios. What if someone took her? What if she didn't leave by choice? What if that damn letter is just a distraction?

My heart races with fury. If someone hurt her, and I mean, if they laid even one finger on my woman, I'll burn this city down. I'll make whoever's responsible wish they'd never been born. She's mine, and no one gets to take her from me.

I grab my phone again and call Danielle's phone. No answer. I call again. Again. Again and again.

Each time, I reach her voicemail.

With each call, my breathing grows more ragged. I'm one missed call away from filing a report, tracking her phone, kicking in every door between here and L.A. if I have to.

I continue to dial her number. And then—

"David..."

"Danielle?" My voice is hoarse, like I've been screaming even though I haven't said a word.

There's a barely audible sniffle on the other end. "Hey."

Relief floods my chest so fast it almost knocks the air from my lungs. My knees nearly give out at the sound of her voice. She sounds fragile, like something has broken inside her. "Danielle," I breathe, softer this time. "Are you okay? Where are you? I've been worried sick. I got your note, and I... I didn't know what to think."

"I—I had to," she says, her voice barely holding steady. "I couldn't breathe, David. I felt... caged in."

"Caged?" I repeat, my heart twisting. "Danielle, come on... you know you can talk to me. About anything."

"I do know that," she murmurs. "I always have."

I drag a hand over my face, pacing. "We were talking about marriage. About building a life together. A family. How do we go from that to this?"

She hesitates, and then, with a shaky breath, she says, "That's what scared me, David. All of it. The future we

22

planned as two married and successful lawyers with a family started feeling like it was closing in around me. I didn't know how to say it without disappointing you, without shattering everything we dreamed up."

My chest tightens, but I let her speak.

"I love you... but I'm overwhelmed. Law school. Expectations. You. Me. Marriage. Kids. It's all just... so much. And the truth is... I don't know what I want. Not yet. I only know this—if I stayed, I'd be pretending. And you don't deserve a half-truth version of me."

"Well, congratulations on finally telling your truth," I bite out, anger breaking through the numbness. "You left me here thinking something *happened* to you. I was ready to flip the whole damn city upside down if I didn't hear from you."

"I didn't think you'd freak out like that."

"You left a *note*, Danielle! That's not you. You don't just walk out without a word. I thought—God, I thought someone might've taken you. I thought you were dead."

"I'm sorry," she says through tears. "I just... I couldn't tell you to your face. I needed to go before I lost the nerve, so I didn't even bring all of my things. As soon as I got the nerve to leave, I grabbed my jacket, tossed a few things inside a bag and left."

"Where are you going, Danielle?"

"I have an art residency in California. I leave tomorrow."

My heart doesn't shatter this time. It's just a dull, settled ache, the kind that sinks deep and stays. "Hold on. I couldn't have heard you right. You have a what?"

"An art residency. I have decided to put my artistry talents to work."

I can't believe what I'm hearing. Everything we dreamed together about passing the bar, opening a firm, and building a life that blended our passions wasn't real. The dreams were mine. Not ours. They were mine alone. And alone is what I am right now. She let me carry our pretend future on my back while she created another reality in secret.

All those late nights, all those whispered promises about being like her father, about wanting this life with me. Were they lies? Or just dreams she outgrew without telling me?

"I would have supported you in doing that had you been honest."

"David, I—"

I cut her off. "You already made your choice," I say quietly, the words heavy in my throat. "And I guess I have to be okay with that." My voice softens, nearly breaking. "Besides, you were leaving long before you packed a bag."

All the fight drains out of me. What's left is just... emptiness.

"David..."

"You don't have to say anything else." I swallow hard. "Just... take care of yourself."

"I never stopped loving you," she says, and it feels like a punch to the chest.

I close my eyes. "Apparently, our love wasn't enough."

I end the call before I can let myself care what else she has to say. The phone drops from my hand to the counter with a quiet thud. Her note is still sitting there like it's saying 'fuck you David.'

I grab it, crumple it in my fist, and toss it into the trash.

Then, I sit on the same stool I bought with her, in the apartment we made plans in, and I let her absence and the betrayal I never saw coming hit me.

Danielle is gone, and I let myself feel it.

"Almost.

It's a big word for me.

I feel it everywhere.

Almost home.

Almost happy.

Almost changed.

Almost, but not quite.

Not yet.

Soon, maybe."

– Joan Bauer

Chapter Three

Maya

Time Changes Things

Three Years Later

Man, I remember when owning my own boutique was nothing but a late-night, wish-on-a-star kind of dream. Back then, it was just me, a notebook full of ideas, and way too many sleepless nights imagining my designs on some wide-eyed bride, grinning ear to ear. I never thought I'd actually get here, much less be here, living it on repeat. Even though I lost some people that I loved along the way, Dreamy Wedding Bridal Boutique is not just a business; it's a whole life-changer.

But let me tell you, I wouldn't be standing here if it weren't for Olivia and Jasmine. I met them at this wedding expo, and we clicked like we'd known each other forever. One minute, we're swapping ideas; the next, we're mapping out plans to open this boutique in Azalea Cove, a little gem of a city just outside Atlanta. It wasn't easy; I left a six figure corporate job and lost my man in the process but look at me now—a successful woman bosspreneur doing the damn thing.

At this very moment, though, standing beside a soon-to-be bride in *my* shop, the air scented with jasmine and vanilla (it's supposed to calm people down, emphasis on "supposed to"), I can't help but wonder what I was thinking some days.

"What were you guys thinking when you installed the lighting in here? It's too bright!" the Bridezilla barks, snapping me right out of my thoughts. Her voice is so sharp, it could cut through the tulle we just steamed. "It's so horrible that I can't see how this dress looks on me! It's practically glowing like a ghost's sheet," she fusses.

I don't even flinch. Years in this business have taught me how to smile through chaos. *It's not the lighting,* I want to say. *It's your body enhancements and attitude.* But do I say that to her? No, because professionalism. Always professionalism.

I press my lips together, resisting the urge to point out that the lighting is perfect. It's her butt implant, attitude, and maybe even her contact prescription that needs adjusting. Instead, I smooth my voice and smile. "We can adjust the lighting slightly, but the mirrors give a true reflection. Let's focus on how the gown fits. The alterations team has done an amazing job."

"Amazing?" she shrieks, tugging at the beaded bodice like it personally insulted her. "Do you see this? It's cutting into my ribs! And these beads? What even are these? I specifically said I wanted pearls to fall down over my hips. And I meant *real* pearls. Are you even listening to me?"

Oh, I've been listening, alright. I've been listening since the first time she walked through the door, acting like she's auditioning for her own reality show. And let me tell you, there *are* pearls on this dress. They are the *exact* pearls she picked out from the swatches. But she doesn't just want pearls. She wants the whole damn ocean, delivered on a silver platter by mermaids.

I take a deep breath. Short, continuous inhales and exhales. In. Out. In. Out. Because Lord knows, I didn't work this hard to build this boutique just to end up catching a case over a bridezilla.

As if sensing my rising blood pressure, Jasmine's voice floats from the backroom, cool and calm. "Maya, everything okay out there?"

For a split second, I want to shout, *Hell no, come get this Bridezilla before I pull a Tamela Mann and take her ass to the king!* But no. I don't go there because professionalism. Always professionalism.

"I've got it!" I call back, my voice just a little too chipper to be real.

Got it is a stretch. Between her nonstop whining and this headache knocking like it wants to come inside, I feel like a loose thread on a beaded gown, ready to snap any second. I roll my shoulders back, adjust my stance, and plaster on my customer-service smile. In my mind, I'm repeating my mantra: Professionalism. Always professionalism.

That is... until the door chimes.

In strolls a dark-skinned man who I'm convinced the word king was created for, draped in a suit so sharp it could cut glass. The way he carries himself exhibits straight-up royalty. His suit is custom-made to fit every inch of his frame just right. His smooth dark skin practically glows under the boutique lighting, and his dark wavy hair is lined up perfectly. Not a strand out of place. He's giving off major Mufasa vibes, walking in like he owns everything in sight. The leather briefcase he's carrying means business all by itself, even if nothing else in the room does.

Everything about this man screams out of place in the boutique. He's definitely not a groom. He doesn't even spare a glance at the racks of dreamy tulle and lace that usually make people stop and stare. Nope, his eyes lock straight on me, like I'm the only thing in the room worth noticing. And damn if that look doesn't send heat traveling down my spine.

My fingers tighten slightly on the satin fabric I'm adjusting. My pulse betrays me for half a second. I gather myself, because no....I don't do this. I don't get thrown off by a man walking into my shop looking like a Wall Street fantasy wrapped in melanin and ambition. As far as I know, he could be somebody's future husband. But there's something about the confidence in his stride, the way he carries that briefcase like it holds the blueprint to running the world, that makes me momentarily forget how to act.

I square my shoulders, shaking off whatever ridiculous momentary lapse in professionalism I just had. He's probably just another smooth talker, trying to sell us something for the boutique that we don't need.

"Yeah, we're good. Not looking to add anything new right now," I say, cutting him off before he can hit me with some sales pitch about the next big thing in the bridal industry.

He lifts a brow like my comment didn't even register. "You're Maya Thompson," he says, his voice smooth but with just enough bite to let me know he's not here to sell me anything.

I blink, caught off guard. "That's me," I reply, trying to keep my tone neutral. The last thing I need is one more person demanding my attention today.

"David Coleman," he says, offering a firm handshake. His grip is solid, just like his tone, which is also warm, secure, and sizzling in my spirit just a second longer than necessary. "I'm here about the wedding agreements for Amiri Knox's fiancée, the soon-to-be Tess Knox. There are a few details in the contracts I need to go over."

Details immediately flood my mind about Tess Knox's wedding. That ceremony's not even on the calendar for months. And the contracts are already tighter than a bridesmaid dress two sizes too small. They have been approved by both his lawyers and mine. What could he possibly have to go over?

"You want to go over them *now*? What's the issue?" I ask, raising an eyebrow, trying to figure out if this man is serious.

"There are a few discrepancies in the timeline and accessory guarantees that I need to clarify, so now is good," he says with that same clipped, matter-of-fact tone, like he's dropping some life-or-death legal bombshell.

Bridezilla clears her throat, loud enough to make her presence felt. "Excuse me? I was here first. I know you don't think I'm about to wait for you two to have a meeting!" Her words drip with entitlement, and I already know she's about to make this ten times worse.

I hold up a hand toward her, my smile polite but barely holding. "One moment, please," I say through gritted teeth before turning back to *Mr. Coleman*. "As you can see, I'm currently in the middle of a fitting. If you'd like to leave your number, I can reach out when I'm free."

That should've been the end of it. A normal person would take the hint. But not him. He doesn't move an inch.

Instead, he calmly pulls a folder out of his leather briefcase like he's a magician about to dazzle me with a thrilling new act called 'More Paperwork and Wasting Your Time.'

"This won't take long," he says, unbothered. "It's important that we finalize these details today."

I blink, stunned by the audacity of this man. I don't know if it's the suit, the briefcase, or just his general vibe, but he clearly thinks he owns my time. Meanwhile, I'm standing here wondering how I can get away with telling him and Bridezilla what I think about their demands.

My smile is tight, controlled, and just this side of polite. "Today? As in right-now today?" I ask in disbelief. "Surely, you can see I'm a little busy."

He glances at Bridezilla, who's now tapping her velvet glass-manicured nails against the counter like an impatient villain. Then, he looks back at me, his gaze piercing a hole through my skin. It's so commanding it sends a slow heat curling through my stomach.

"Which is why this needs to be handled quickly," he insists, his voice dropping to a low, velvety timbre, rich with authority. "The sooner we're done, the sooner you can get back to your bride."

He's serious. Completely serious. And worse, that voice is deep, smooth, and laced with just enough testosterone to make my pulse jump.

Before I can even piece together a response that isn't, *You've lost your damn mind,* Jasmine steps out from the backroom followed by Olivia. Jasmine's brow furrows as she takes in the scene: Bridezilla looking like she's about to throw a tantrum, me trying not to throw hands with her, and Mr. David Coleman standing there like he owns our building.

Olivia, ever observant, leans casually and David.

I let out a long sigh, gesturing toward Mr. Too-against the doorframe, a cup of coffee in hand and an amused eyebrow raised. "What's going on?" Olivia asks, her tone casual but her eyes sharp as they roam between me Much-Time-On-His-Hands. "Apparently, contracts for a wedding months away can't wait. Today is the day they must be reviewed," I say, my voice dripping with sarcasm. "He's here to go over timelines and accessory guarantees for the Knox contract... again." I emphasize the last word because, really, this is ridiculous.
Jasmine steps forward, her voice calm and professional, which is the total opposite of how I'm feeling right now. "Hello, David. Can I—"

"No," he cuts her off, snappy and to the point, like he's handing out free attitude to anyone who wants some. His gaze darkens as he looks at her with piercing eyes. "Didn't expect to see you again, Jasmine."

Jasmine doesn't even flinch. "Same, David, but I can go over the contracts with you and take care of what you need done today."

"Actually..." David's eyes lock with mine. "I'd prefer to go over them with the person who originally put the contract together with my team. Leads to less confusion."

Translation: He's trying to ruin my day.

Jasmine shoots me a quick look, and I see a crack in her composure. It's apparent she knows David, and their relationship isn't good.

Olivia, always the peacemaker, steps in smooth as ever. "Alright, sir," she says, her tone cool with just enough bite to be taken seriously, "how about we set up a time for you and Maya to meet? She's with a client right now, and if we lock in a meeting, she can give you her undivided attention."

You'd think this would be the part where he nods, sets up a meeting time, and walks out the door like a normal person. But nope.

He doesn't so much as blink. "I appreciate the suggestion, but I'd rather see her now. This will only take ten minutes."

Olivia raises an eyebrow, taking a slow sip of her coffee before responding. "Ten minutes is a quick meeting. If it's only a few details like that, Jasmine or I'd be happy to help."

David doesn't spare a glance at Jasmine. "I would prefer to go over the details with Maya, the person who originally set up the contract," he reiterates as if whatever we're going to talk about will single-handedly save the world from all future wedding catastrophes.

Before I can fire back, Bridezilla cuts in, her patience fully on E. "Speaking of details! Can we focus on *my* details? I'm sure you can all see that I'm the only bride here! The fuck," Her voice cuts through the air like a nail on a chalkboard, dragging my headache up another notch.

I take a deep, calming breath, pushing back the rising frustration.

You got this, Maya.

Professional.

Always professional.

"Jasmine, can you take over this fitting? Olivia, can you grab me the client agreement binder?" My voice is calm, but I'm practically willing them to tag me out of this mess.

Jasmine nods, stepping toward Bridezilla with her signature calm, empathetic energy. "I know you've been working with Maya, so I'll just help her out until she finishes her meeting. Let's take a closer look at the bodice and see how we can make this feel more comfortable," she says, smoothly redirecting Bridezilla's meltdown into something manageable.

Olivia, on the other hand, gives me a subtle wink, like she's saying *good luck,* before disappearing to the back.

And just like that, it's me and *Mr. Coleman* locked in a stare down.

"Let's get this over with," I say, grabbing a pen from the counter and guiding him to my office.

He lays out his folder on my desk with the kind of precision that makes me want to say to hell with the folder and the spreadsheets that rode in with it. Instead, I proceed with listening attentively to his calm and firm tone. "I reviewed the delivery timeline," he starts. "The contract specifies delivery by two weeks prior to the wedding, but the vendor schedule I received shows it arriving a week later. That's cutting it too close for the bride."

As he starts explaining his concerns, I'm trying to stay annoyed, but my eyes catch on something, and I hate myself a little for it. It's the way his hands move, strong and deliberate, the veins running along his knuckles as he flips through the pages.

It's also the way his suit jacket pulls just enough to hint at strong arms and broad shoulders. Then there's his voice. Deep, smooth, with just the right amount of rasp, like it was designed to slide under my skin and make me forget about my dignity. His voice doesn't fill the room; it takes its time and settles into it. *Why does it have to sound like it's trying to make my panties reconsider their loyalty?*

Blinking hard, I snap myself out of whatever that was.

Focus, Maya. This is a man with the personality of a spreadsheet. There is no way he's got your mind spinning.

But I can't help it. He's aggravating, yes. He's probably just like Troy, only focused on his career and couldn't care less what a woman wants. He's also... so damn unfortunately attractive. Why is it always the annoying ones that get me worked up?

"And that's why this particular delivery timeline needs to be adjusted," David finishes, glancing up from his folder like he's daring me to challenge him.

I clear my throat, forcing myself to ignore the tug of attraction I'm fighting to suppress. Focus, Maya. "All of your concerns were already addressed in the amended timeline we sent to your assistant," I finally respond.

"True, but I want the contract to reflect the changes. Keeps everyone honest."

I arch a brow and lean back slightly. "You really don't trust us to handle this, do you?"

That smirk of his is quick and subtle, but it lands like a power move, not just an expression. "I'm not saying I don't trust you. It's just that getting every detail right reflects on me. And remember, I don't miss."

Of course, *that's* his answer. Mr. Perfect Lawyer, aka *Mr. I-Don't-Miss.* The confidence in his voice is enough to make me roll my eyes, but something about the way he smirks feels personal like it's aimed at me.

I straighten my shoulders, not about to let him throw me off my game. "Well, Mr. I-Don't-Miss, everything you're pointing out was already addressed."

"And yet, I'm here because it's not reflected in the contract I'm holding," he replies smoothly, like his very presence is all the justification he needs.

I shake my head. "Fine," I say, glancing up at him with a forced smile. "We'll send over a revised contract detailing the delivery verbatim to what we have in our timeline. As mentioned earlier, the updated delivery timeline was sent to your assistant, Yolexis Graham, I think is her name. So, I'm warning you, if you find one more 'discrepancy' that's not really a discrepancy, I'm charging you an hourly rate for wasting my time."

His smirk widens just a fraction like he's enjoying this way more than he should. "Fair enough."

I sigh and lean back slightly. "Is that all?" I ask, feeling overwhelmed by being in his presence and already mentally scheduling a nap.

He pauses, studying me for a moment longer than necessary, like he's trying to figure something out. Finally, he nods. "That's all for now."

With that, he gathers his things, snapping his folder shut with that same meticulous precision that somehow makes me want to scream and swoon at the same time. He heads for the door with an air of confidence that practically announces its exit. Just before stepping out, he pauses.

Slowly, he turns back to me, his eyes holding mine for just a second too long. With a smirk that's equal parts cocky and devastating, he lifts his chin slightly. Then, just to make sure he stays in my head for the rest of the day, he winks.

"Nice meeting you, Maya Thompson," he says over his shoulder, his voice smooth as ever. And just like that, he's gone.

I let out a deep exhale and roll my eyes at the door. The traitorous little flip in my stomach is a problem. A whole damn problem.

When I make it back to the front of the boutique, Jasmine walks over to stand beside me. "Just so you know, David and I went on a blind date once."

"How could you stand him?" I ask.

"I couldn't. That's why I didn't go for a second date. He seemed caught up on himself," she blurts out.

I smirk. "Well, he *does* have that 'I wake up to a mirror and wink at myself' energy."

I brush invisible lint off my blouse like it'll help me reset from the annoyingly irresistibleness of David Coleman. I glance around, relieved to notice that Bridezilla has finally left. "Ambrosia left?" I ask, focusing on something else.

"Yep, Bridezilla is gone," Jasmine replies, following my gaze to the fitting area. "I was able to settle her down long enough for her to give another list of requests for her dress."

I exhale like we just survived a war zone. "She'll be back with an army of complaints and unrealistic demands next week."

Jasmine chuckles softly. "As long as she brings in her football player fiancé's money with her, we will listen to her complaints. Besides, at least you won't have the sexy lawyer in the suit to distract you. He was very intense today."

"I definitely picked up on that." I roll my eyes. "Let's hope I never have Bridezilla on one side and Mr. Intense on the other ever again in life."

"He may be annoying," Olivia chimes in, walking from the back office with two coffees, one of which she hands to me. She leans casually against the counter, sipping hers. "But he's undoubtedly fine with some big energy. Honey, I offered to handle him for you, but I don't know if I would have been able to do it ... whew!"

I shrug. "I didn't notice all of that."

She tilts her head, giving me that I know you saw it too side-eye. "I don't know how you didn't notice it. He's fine as wine. Like, the kind of fine that should be illegal in multiple states."

Jasmine nods, tapping her nails against the counter. "Mmhmm. Intense, fine, and completely aware of both. Maybe he'll show you a different side of him than what he showed me. I could definitely tell that he was interested in what he saw."

"You dated him?" Olivia chimes in.

"Girl, yes!" Jasmine responds. "And he had the personality of a cardboard that really was in love with cardboard."

"In love with himself?" Olivia questions.

"At least, that's what I picked up about him. But it's safe to say, he's fine and for the right woman he might not be so self-absorbed."

I take a sip of my coffee, hoping it'll cool down the heat creeping up my neck. "Y'all finished or you done?" I ask, channeling my inner-most Birdman spirit.

Olivia laughs. "I don't know. Are you? Because there is no way I would let that one get away without testing his intensity."

I raise an eyebrow, taking another sip of my coffee. "I'm not trying to test him for anything. I just wanted him out of here like what T.I. said, expeditiously."

Olivia crosses her arms, leaning against the counter. "So, what exactly did he want? He had all those papers like he was serving subpoenas or something."

"He wanted to update the contract to match the amended timeline agreement," I reply, my tone dismissive. "Apparently, it's 'just to keep everyone honest.' Whatever that means."

"Well, if it's just that, I can handle it and get our lawyers to review it again," Olivia offers. "I know you have a lot going on with Ambrosia."

"The correct name for her is Bridezilla. She has earned that title," Jasmine corrects.

"She really has earned it," I chuckle. "But nope. I've got it. I can handle her, and I can handle David," I say.

Olivia's brow arches, and Jasmine smirks.

"Uh-huh. You've *got it*, huh?" Olivia asks, her voice dripping with amusement. "And here I thought you couldn't wait to get him out of your hair."

I roll my eyes. "I just want it done right since I went over the entire agreement with him again. That's all."

Jasmine chuckles, shaking her head. "Maya, if I didn't know better, I'd think you *want* to deal with the lawyer again. Maybe he'll be at the Governors Ball in a few weeks."

"I hope not," I shoot back, grabbing a clipboard as if the act itself can shut down the conversation. "I don't have time for his nonsense."

"Sure," Olivia says, grinning. "Whatever you say, Maya. Sounds like you're making time for his nonsense to me. Maybe you should invite him as your plus one to the Govenor's Ball, an event I'm looking forward to by the way." She starts shaking her hips and dancing to the beat of her own music.

I wave her off, rolling my eyes. "Uh, no ma'am. I will not be inviting him as my plus anything. Besides, I keep forgetting all about that ball. It's going to sneak up on me, and I won't be ready."

Olivia shakes her head. "Oh, no. We're not letting you miss this one. If I have to come over there and get you dressed myself, you are going."

"Okay, okay..."

~*~

Hours later, we're all in our zones working on different projects. Meanwhile, I'm still thinking about David. Not in a *feeling him like that* kind of way.

No, no, no.

Definitely not feeling him.

Maybe, I'm thinking about his well-fitted suit, the smirk, or the wink. Or the way his voice melts into my senses and renders me defenseless. Or how his razor-sharp tongue made it impossible for me to win an argument because I was thinking about all the things he could do with said tongue.

Ugh. "I need to get it together," I mutter under my breath. "Why am I like this? I'm not looking for love, but something about him is making me think like this."

Chapter Four

David

Little Firecracker

The GPS chirps out instructions, but I'm not paying attention. My mind is elsewhere. I shouldn't be doing this. I should be at my downtown Atlanta office, pouring over Turner Enterprises' new venture line by line, locking down every clause. Doing so may prevent me from getting a call from the owner with any concerns he spots. The Turner Enterprises contract is the kind of deal that could be scrutinized under a microscope. It demands my focus, my full attention.

Yet I'm back in Azalea Cove, sitting here in the parking lot at a wedding boutique, preparing to go over a revised contract that clarifies the dates the dress, shoes and accessories will be delivered for Tess.

My jaw ticks as I grip the steering wheel. What in the actual hell am I doing? An assistant or junior associate at the firm should be handling these simple contract

47

revisions. This isn't something a partner at a prestigious law firm should be personally overseeing.

But last week, I was flipping through *Elite Bridal Magazine,* strictly for business, of course, when I saw her. Maya Thompson stood there with her business partners in a spread about top Black-owned bridal boutiques, looking like she belonged on the cover of *Forbes* and *Vogue* at the same damn time. I recognized the boutique's name immediately. *Dreamy Weddings.* Some of our high-profile clients signed deals with them for full-scale wedding packages.

Seeing her in the magazine should've been the end of it, but something about her wouldn't let me leave it at that.

She stood out amongst her friends, especially one I recognized from a blind date that still makes me cringe. Jasmine. She was cool, smart, beautiful... but I wasn't even really there emotionally that night. I'd gone out with her during a vulnerable time after Danielle left. I wasn't looking for connection. I was looking to feel like I still had control. Like I was still desirable and worthy.

So, I spent the entire evening talking about myself. I didn't ask her about her life, her dreams. Hell, I don't even remember what she ordered. The truth is, I wasn't talking to Jasmine that night; I was talking to Danielle. I was trying to prove something to someone who wasn't even in the room.

Maya is different.

Just looking at her picture makes me lose my good sense. In the magazine photo, she's confidence personified, standing in front of her boutique like she laid every single brick herself. That drive, that fire in her eyes, that smirk on her lips that dares the world to question her value... it pulls me in and matches my energy.

I tried to forget her picture and our first meeting. I should be in my office working on million-dollar contracts, but there's something about her that I can't walk away from. That's why I'm sitting in my car, in front of her boutique... again.

I tell myself this is all about Amiri and Tess's wedding contracts. Lexington Enterprises hired my firm to make sure every detail is perfect, so I'm just making sure we're on track. But this second trip? Off the top, I know this has nothing to do with the agreement and everything to do with the mocha-skinned temptation wrapped in attitude who runs this place.

"Maya Thompson," I mutter, shaking my head. After one meeting last week, that woman didn't just get under my skin; she camped out there, set up shop, and refused to leave. I've had intrusive thoughts about her all through the day, every day, since the day I saw her.

As if to remind me of my priorities as a lawyer, my phone buzzes in the cupholder. The name on the screen belongs to Atlanta's richest man, Jacob Turner, the billionaire real estate mogul who almost singlehandedly keeps Coleman and Williams Law Group at the top echelon of law practices in Georgia.

"Mr. Turner," I answer smoothly, putting the car in park and leaning back in my seat.

"Coleman," Turner starts with his voice ragged, "Reviewing the updated terms for the X-Tex government building contract reveals a few things we need to revisit. I don't want any loopholes that could leave us exposed to liability."

"Of course," I reply, keeping my tone steady but firm. "I'm finalizing it now but go ahead and shoot me an email with the specific areas raising red flags. I'll triple-check them, and there will be no cracks or weak points. We won't miss anything."

"You know that's what I like to hear," Turner says, his voice dipping with warning, "but I'm getting a little concerned, especially with the Agatha trial looming."

I sit up straighter. "There's no need for concern," I say, sharper this time. "You'll have a full rundown on your desk by end of business. As far as the Agatha attempt at a money grab, we're going to prevail in showing they have no ground to stand on."

"I hear you, but this X-Tex deal's too big to slip up on," he presses.

"I don't do slip-ups," I fire back. Then I seal it with my signature: "We won't miss."

By all means, I should be headed back to my office to get on top of his concerns. But as the call ends, my eyes drift back to the boutique entrance.

I call my assistant. "Yolexis, be on the lookout for documents being faxed over from Turner."

"I'm on it."

As the call ends, the irony isn't lost on me. Turner expects me to be laser-focused on his multi-million-dollar deal, yet here I am, parked outside a bridal shop, eyes locked on the door and floral-filled windows, knowing the woman I can't get out of my head is on the other side. I can already hear the question forming in the back of my head: *What the hell are you doing, David?*

I tell myself this is just good client service. Amiri Knox is a high-profile figure in the Lexington Enterprise circle, and his wedding is practically a corporate event. I can't afford to leave anything to chance. I also can't afford to let *her* distract me.

Still, I take a deep breath, step out of the car, and straighten my suit jacket. I tell myself it's just business. That's all I'm here for.

The boutique smells like jasmine and vanilla when I step inside. The whole vibe is warm and inviting. The lighting is soft, bouncing off walls lined with pristine white gowns and sparkling accessories. It's beautiful in a way I don't have the bandwidth to appreciate. My focus is on locating her as I scan the boutique.

51

And there she is.

Maya Thompson stands near a display of accessories, her head tilted slightly as she adjusts a row of pearls on a velvet board. Her fingers move with care. She's deliberate and precise. It's clear to see she doesn't just arrange things; she *curates* them. She steps back to assess her work, and her expression momentarily softens into something almost... peaceful.

I clear my throat, and her head snaps up.

The moment she spots me, the softness disappears. Her brows pinch together, her lips press into a line, and I can see the tension flooding her body like she's preparing for battle.

"You're back?" she says, crossing her arms, her voice sharp enough to cut through the boutique's serene atmosphere.

There's no hiding the irritation on her face, and I can't say I blame her. She was all in her creative zone, and here I am, unexpectedly pulling her out to go over lines of paperwork, all because I want to see her again.

"Good to see you too, Ms. Thompson," I reply, letting a small smirk tug at my lips.

"I didn't hear the door chime."

"I figured you didn't with how engrossed you were in your work. I'm here for a follow-up regarding Tess's package."

"Of course you are," she mutters, more to herself than to me, but the way her lips press into a thin line tells me I've already gotten under her skin.

Good, that makes two of us.

She takes steps toward me. The click of her heels bringing her toward me sends heat down my spine. The way she moves confidently and self-assured commands every drop of my attention. And don't get me started on those thick-ass thighs, flexing with each step like they were made to test my discipline.

"I sent a newly signed version of the contract and dates to you and your assistant's email," she says, her tone dry. "Was something missing?"

I snap out of the trance her thighs have me in and pull a folder from my briefcase with practiced ease. Her eyes flick to the folder like it's the enemy. "There are still a few details that need clarifying."

Her brow lifts, and a tiny arch makes one side rise just a bit higher than the other. A small crease forms between her eyes, showing her annoyance. And it's sexy as hell.

"Details?" she repeats. "What kind of details need to be clarified? Surely, ordering a dress and accessories is not this complicated."

I shrug. "I received the amended contract. But there are still a few things that seem a little off, and I want to make sure there are no liabilities."

Her lips press together tightly like she's biting back a response. "Liabilities," she repeats, the word practically dripping with skepticism.

"Don't take it personal. This is just the way I do business," I assure her.

Her laugh is shrilling, humorless, and way too short. "Nothing personal. It's just you've been in here more than most of our brides, Mr. Coleman. I'm starting to think you've got an ulterior motive."

I pause for a minute and study her expression. She's good, and I mean, really good at keeping her face composed, but her eyes betray her. There's something there, just under the surface, slipping through the cracks. I wonder if it's attraction. Or is it curiosity? Maybe she's trying to figure me out as much as I'm trying to figure her out.

"And what motive would that be?" I ask, tilting my head slightly.

She blinks, and her lips part as if she's going to respond. Then, she doesn't. Instead, she lets out a frustrated huff and shakes her head, muttering something I can't quite hear under her breath.

"You didn't answer the question," I press.

She narrows her eyes. "You're awfully persistent, aren't you?"

"It's part of the job," I say, widening my smile to get a reaction out of her.

Her gaze locks onto mine, and we're just... staring at each other, not saying a word, like we're testing who's gonna blink first. The longer we stand here, the clearer it gets that I'll lose this standoff if she doesn't crack soon.

"You know," she finally says, breaking the silence with a tilt of her head, "I don't get it. Most lawyers I've worked with don't sweat the small stuff like you do. They leave that to the wedding planners. You're kind of... different."

"I'll take that as a compliment," I reply, leaning slightly against the counter.

"It wasn't one," she says, but the corner of her mouth twitches, almost like she's fighting a smile.

"Hmm." I tap the folder against the counter lightly. "Maybe I'm just thorough."

"Or maybe you just like getting under my skin," she shoots back, crossing her arms again.

Her tone is biting, but the way she shifts her stance gives her away. She wants me under her skin as much as I want to be under it. God knows I wouldn't mind being under her skin. Hell, I want to be deep in it. Wrapped in her warmth, her thighs locked around me while I get lost in everything she pretends she's not thinking about right now.

I laugh softly, shaking my head, fighting to keep my thoughts in check. "Believe it or not, Ms. Thompson, I don't make a habit of irritating bridal boutique owners."

"Well, congratulations," she says dryly. "You're excelling at something new."

"So, are you always this combative?" I ask, curious now.

"Only when I'm dealing with lawyers who think they can tell me how to run my business," she fires back, raising her perfectly arched brow again. While her tone is sharp, there continues to be a faint, telltale curve at the corner of her lips that doesn't quite match her words.

"Noted," I say with a chuckle, watching how she fiddles with the edge of the clipboard in her hand.

Her eyes peruse the folder I'm holding. "So, what's so urgent and pressing in this contract that one half of Coleman and Williams Law Group had to come here in person again?" she asks.

I set the folder down on the counter between us. "After going through the timeline again, I realized there's a gap. If the shipment gets delayed even by a day, it could interfere with the final fitting schedule." I glance up at her, checking to see if she's following what I'm saying. "When you're dealing with top-dollar clients, you can't leave anything to chance. And me personally, I don't like surprises."

She tilts her head slightly, her brow lifting as she leans one hip against the counter. "Neither do I," she says, her tone quieter. "That's why I'd prefer an email or for you to set up appointments to go over things like this."

"I'll schedule one for my next visit," I reply smoothly, meeting her gaze.

"Your next visit?" she repeats, one eyebrow arching higher than the other.

"You never know what will happen that brings us back together like this," I say, smirking as I slide the folder closer to her. "I always believe it's better to be proactive than reactive."

She stares at me for a moment, her lips pressing into a thin line. "Proactive, huh? So that's why you're here again, looking for a problem before it even exists?"

I shrug. "Call it thoroughness."

"Call it overkill," she mutters under her breath, but loud enough for me to hear.

She lets out a sigh that makes me chuckle. I don't know what it is about her, but she has this way of making you want to be closer to her, even when she's trying to push you away. I'm about to say something else, but the sound of heels clicking toward us interrupts the moment.

"Everything okay out here?" Olivia walks over and inserts herself into the conversation, clipboard in hand. She looks between the two of us, her eyebrows lifting slightly.

"Oh, it's nothing," Maya says quickly, stepping back from the counter. "David here is just making sure I earn my paycheck today," she adds, her tone sprinkled with sarcasm.

Olivia smirks. "It's good to have someone keep us on our toes. Hi David."

I nod. "Hi. How are you today?"

Olivia nods. "I'm good."

"Well, I don't need anyone keeping me on my toes," Maya mutters.

Before I can respond, Jasmine strolls in from the back, sipping on her iced coffee like she doesn't have a care in the world. "What's all this tension?" she asks, raising an eyebrow. "Y'all arguing over satin or chiffon now?"

"Delivery timelines," I say, holding up the folder. "Critical business decisions, according to Mr. Coleman."

Jasmine smirks, giving me a quick once-over. "Well, if the delivery man keeps showing up looking like *that*, we might need to create a standing appointment. Could be good for business. Or at least... mildly entertaining."

Maya shoots her a glare so sharp, I almost feel it.

Jasmine shrugs, unbothered. "What? Don't look at me like that. I only went on one date with the man. It was weird. He spent the whole night talking about himself and law and didn't notice when I checked out." She turns to Maya, grinning. "He's all yours, sis."

I point to Maya and say, "Exactly. I'm your problem now. You should listen to your friends."

Maya gives Jasmine a death glare and then shifts her fury to me. "Mr. Coleman, why don't we go to the back office so we can go over these details one last time to make sure every line is correct. Then, we can stay out of each other's hair. How about that?"

She puts an emphasis on last time, which causes me to bite down on my bottom lip to stop myself from saying this is far from the last time we will see each other.

"Yeah... last time," I say under my breath.

She turns and starts walking toward the back, and the rhythmic sway of her hips puts me in a chokehold. The way she carries herself is confident, yet soft and feminine. I think I'm in love with her walk all by itself.

We reach her office, which is small and cozy, tucked neatly behind a wall of bridal inventory. The scent of jasmine lingers in the air even here. She gestures to the chair across from her desk, where a few neatly stacked binders sit waiting.

I place the binders on the corner of her desk and take a seat, leaning back slightly as she moves around to the other side of the desk. She doesn't relax. She sits on the edge of her chair like she's poised for another round of debate. She flips open one of the binders as though this whole interaction is just an annoying box she needs to check off her to-do list.

"Well?" she prompts, arching a brow. "I don't have time to waste. Let's get this contract as tight as possible, for once and for all."

As we go through the details, I find myself less focused on the documents and more on her. The way her dark, silky brows furrow slightly when she reads through the fine print. The way her fingers tap impatiently on the edge of the paper as I make her double-check something. The way the light catches on her mocha skin, softening her features, making her look like the kind of dream you don't want to wake up from.

"Can you confirm this again?" I ask, pointing to one of the guarantees.

She huffs softly, but I catch it. "We already went over this," she mutters, flipping to the corresponding section in the binder anyway. "Everything's outlined about the delivery for the shoes as plain as day."

"I like to be thorough," I say, leaning back in my chair as I watch her.

"And I like not wasting my time," she snaps.

I have millions of dollars' worth of contracts back at my office downtown that need my attention, so I probably should leave and give her some of her time back, but something keeps me here. Some small part of me enjoys seeing the way she can't quite hide how I'm getting to her.

Maya goes over the last line of our agreement and closes the binder with a loud thud. She sits back in her chair and asks, "Now that we are guaranteeing a week earlier delivery and fitting for your bride, will there be anything else, Mr. Coleman?" Her eyes lock onto mine, challenging me to find another reason to be in her space.

I pause, staring at her before shaking my head. "No, I think we've covered everything."

"Good," she says sharply, standing and gathering the paperwork. "Then, I think we're done."

"Thank you for your time, Ms. Thompson," I say as I rise from my seat.

"You're welcome, Mr. Coleman. I trust that you have everything you need now?"

"For now," I reply, chuckling under my breath as I head for the door. "Thanks for your cooperation."

"Sure," she says, crossing her arms.

As I walk out into the boutique with Maya trailing close behind me, Jasmine and Olivia exchange one of those looks of amusement or mischief; I can't decipher which. Maya catches it too and groans like she already knows what's coming.

"What?" she demands in a whisper.

"Nothing," Jasmine says, her grin betraying the lie.

"It's just... you two seem very *dedicated* to those contracts," Olivia adds, her tone dripping with playful sarcasm.

Maya shoots them a death glare, waving her hand like she's swatting at flies. "Shhh. At least wait until he leaves."

I smirk, catching the slightest blush creeping onto her face.

"Goodbye, Mr. Coleman," she calls after me in a biting tone, like she's trying to convince her girls I don't have her spiraling.

But I know better. I might not have been the man for Jasmine, but I can feel it in my bones that I could be the man Maya needs.

"Goodbye, Ms. Thompson," I say over my shoulder with a smug grin as I push the door open. I don't look back, but somehow, I know she's still watching.

The warm air hits my face when I step outside. That's when I realize I'm smiling like some fool who didn't just spend half an hour "debating" bridal wear details. Something about her has me willing to jump over the ledge and into whatever I can get into with her. She's beautiful, smart, stubborn, and has this energy that keeps me on my toes. It's like a magnetic force I can't quite shake.

"Having tight contracts is the goal," I tell myself as I slide into my car and start the engine. *It has nothing to do with her. Absolutely nothing.*

I pull out of the lot, and my mind doesn't go to the millions of things I have to do today. It goes straight back to her. Maya Thompson, standing there with her arms crossed, her eyes daring me to say the wrong thing. And those legs... those thighs. Strong, thick, and speaking for themselves like their own power of attorney.

Gripping the steering wheel, I shake my head. "Get it together, man."

That's going to be hard when the vision of her thighs...I mean, eyes, has already embedded itself in my brain like a song on repeat.

God knows, I need to focus. I have clients, deadlines, and lots of money to make. I have no business thinking about Maya Thompson, the little firecracker that has my attention.

But damn. For the second week in a row, she's lit a fire in me.

Chapter Five

Maya

Call Him Chaos

The door chime jingles, and thankfully, one of my favorite brides-to-be breezes into the shop like a whirlwind. Tess has a garment bag slung over her arm, and her phone is pressed to her ear. Her showing up a few minutes early saves me from spending another extra moment with Bridezilla. Even though David Coleman has gotten on my last nerve about her contracts, I simply adore Tess.

I hand Ambrosia her receipt. "My next appointment is here. Call me if you need anything else."

"How about you call me when I can come and pick up my orders, so I can be done with you all?" Ambrosia barks.

"Will do," I say with a pasted-on smile. Because if I tell her what I'm thinking, I won't be exuding professionalism, and it's always professionalism.

Ambrosia stalks out of the room, flinging her hair over her shoulder like she's God's greatest gift to brides.

Tess, in contrast, radiates warmth. Her smile is bright despite the stress I can see in her posture. "Okay, I'll call you later," she says into her phone before shoving it into her purse. She drops the garment bag on the counter with exaggerated flair. "Maya, I need you to save my sanity today," she announces, half-laughing, but there's something in her voice that doesn't match the energy of her words. "Please tell me this fitting won't take long because my life is pure chaos right now."

I arch a brow, watching her carefully as she catches her breath. "Chaos is a big word for someone who usually floats in here like she's got it all together."

"Trust me, I'm barely floating," she mutters, running a hand through her perfectly styled hair. "Let's just say wedding planning isn't nearly as glamorous as Instagram makes it look. But I can't wait to see how the dress looks with the new adjustments."

I grab her gown from the back and lead her to the fitting area. A few minutes later, she steps onto the fitting platform in front of the mirror, and I notice the tension in her shoulders and slight downturn of her lips. After working with hundreds of brides over the years, I know when someone's working hard to mask their emotions. I can usually tell the difference between wedding stress and something deeper.

"You okay?" I ask, smoothing the fabric at her waist.

"Yeah, I'm fine," she says quickly, waving me off. "Just, you know, wedding stuff. It's a lot."

I nod, giving her space to talk if she wants to. "Planning a wedding can be the perfect way to lose your mind."

"That's why I'm so lucky to have you! You have really helped me keep it together," Tess chuckles, but it doesn't feel genuine as she glances at me in the mirror. Her reflection looks smaller than I've ever seen from her. "It's just— nevermind."

"What is it?" I pause, mid-adjustment.

"It's Marissa."

"Marissa? Your best friend and maid of honor?"

"Yeah." Tess fiddles with the bracelet on her wrist. "She's been... a lot. I mean, she's been great, don't get me wrong. If it weren't for her there would be no me and Amiri. She introduced me to him, and she's helped with so much of the planning, but sometimes..." She hesitates, biting her lip. "Sometimes it feels like she's more excited about this wedding than I am."

I watch her carefully, noting the way she twists her bracelet around her wrist. A nervous tic. A tell. Tess is usually so full of energy, so confident in her choices, but right now, there's something fragile in her voice.

"More excited than you?" I repeat gently, giving her space to elaborate.

She exhales sharply, like she's frustrated with herself for even acknowledging her feelings aloud. "She's been my best friend since college. She was there when I thought love wasn't for me. She's the reason I even met Amiri in the first place. And I know she wants the best for me." Tess swallows hard, her fingers going still against the bracelet. "But sometimes... it feels like she's the one walking down the aisle, not me."

I glance at her reflection, meeting her gaze in the mirror. "Have you told her how you feel?"

Tess lets out a dry laugh. "No. Because I don't even know what I'm feeling. It's not like I don't want to get married. I love Amiri. I do." She says it firmly, like she's trying to convince herself as much as me. "But the way Marissa talks about the wedding, the way she makes decisions before I even have a chance to... I don't know. It's weird, right?"

I hesitate, not wanting to push too hard, but the tension in her voice is impossible to ignore. "It's not weird to want to feel like this wedding is *yours*."

Tess nods slowly, considering my words. Then, with a deep breath, she shakes her head. "Maybe I'm just overthinking. It's probably nothing."

The way her voice wavers and her fingers keep picking at her bracelet shows it's something. I don't think it's nothing.

I blink, trying to piece it together. "Something is making you feel this way."

Tess exhales and turns to face me fully, her expression tight with something she's been holding in for too long. "It's like she and Amiri have this bond that I can't touch. He's known her longer than he's known me, they have all these inside jokes, and half the time, when we're out, I feel like I'm the third wheel on my own dates. They talk like I'm not even there sometimes."

I can't hide my reaction. My brows lift. "Damn. That's... not ideal."

She lets out a humorless laugh. "Tell me about it. And it's not just that. Marissa has all these wedding ideas, and it's hard to say no when it feels like she's living vicariously through me."

I tilt my head, studying her. "But do *you* even like her ideas?"

Tess hesitates, then shrugs. "I mean, yeah... but picking out my dress is the only thing I've done completely on my own. And that's only because she was out of town when I found it. It's not like she didn't *want* to be there."

I don't miss the way she explains Marissa's absence as a coincidence that allowed her some freedom with her wedding. I press my lips together, thinking. From everything Tess has said about Marissa, I know she loves her, but something about this revelation feels off.

"There was one night," she starts softly, "about two months ago after we had left what was supposed to be a double date with Marissa and a guy she'd met, but the guy didn't show up. She came alone with us. After that night, I felt bad for her, but I also felt like she would never find anyone if she was always out with us. The need to solidify my relationship with Amiri was heavy on my mind, so I told him when we got home that we needed some time away together. I didn't care where we went; we just needed to reconnect."

"Did you guys take a vacation?"

"No." She shakes her head. "His work schedule didn't allow it, but we did start taking solo dates, trying to get back in sync. It just felt like we weren't as close as we were when he proposed."

My heart aches for her. I know that feeling all too well. That slow drift, that quiet fear of losing something before you even fully have it.

"What did he say when you told him that?" I ask gently.

"He didn't get it at first. Thought everything was fine. But I needed something to show me he wanted to spend the rest of his life with me, and that I wanted to spend mine with him."

I smooth the hem of her gown. "A lot of couples go through this before getting married. It's like a moment of reckoning, figuring out what forever looks like."

I think about Troy, the last man I loved, and how I just knew we would be together forever. How I knew he would love me through thick and thin. How we would forever be down like two flat tires in the hood. And oh, how wrong I was.

"Amiri and I have something special," Tess murmurs, "and I want that something to belong to only us." Her voice drops even lower. "I love my friend, but I don't want to lose sight of my relationship with the man I'm about to marry because she's always there, making our us a threesome."

"That makes sense," I say, my voice softer now.

She exhales. "I almost called off the wedding," she admits, shocking me. "But Amiri called David after our fight, and that's when things started to turn around."

That name stops me. "David?" I ask, raising an eyebrow. "As in Lexington's lawyer, David?"

Tess nods. "Yeah. I had no one to talk to, so I called Lexington's office to speak to the lawyer handling our prenup. That turned out to be the best decision I ever made. David talked to both of us separately. Gave me some advice beyond the agreement. He told me to trust Amiri's love and reminded me not to let fear wreck something good. Honestly... he helped me remember why I fell for Amiri in the first place."

I don't say anything right away. Instead, I try to wrap my head around this version of David as a thoughtful, patient man who actually gives solid advice. Doesn't quite match the clipboard-wielding control freak I've come to know. Albeit a sexy clipboard wielding control freak.

"He even pulled Amiri to the side," Tess goes on. "Told him straight up to set some boundaries with Marissa, make sure I know I'm the priority. And he's been trying, he really has. But..." Her voice wobbles, and she swallows hard. "Marissa doesn't have anybody else. No man, not close to her family. And she's been my rock since forever, through losing my parents, through everything. She's all I have outside of Amiri."

I nod, letting that sink in. "That's a tough spot for anyone to be in. On the one hand, you feel like you're obligated to entertain her. On the other hand, you just want to spend all of your time with the man you love."

"Yeah," Tess murmurs. "I love her. She's my sister in every way that counts. So I get why she clings to me and Amiri. Once we're married, we're all gonna be family. But sometimes... I just want what's *mine*, you know? I want my own space with Amiri, my own bond with him that doesn't have her woven all through it. Right now, it's like we're stuck in this weird-ass triangle, and I don't know how to break out of it."

I straighten up, brushing a stray thread off her dress. "That's a lot to carry."

She lets out a tired laugh. "It is. But I'll figure it out. I have to. Everything's gonna be fine."

I give her a look. "Are you sure?"

"I'm positive."

"Well, just know that you're stronger than you think, Tess. And whenever you need someone to talk to, you know where to find me."

Her eyes soften, and she reaches for my hand, giving it a squeeze. "Thanks for listening, Maya. I didn't plan to say all of that. This was more therapeutic than I expected. Should I be sliding you some cash for a therapy session too?"

I chuckle and pull her in for a quick hug. "Nah, girl, you're good. Just take care of yourself. And I better see you soon."

She starts to step off the platform, but I stop her gently with a hand on her arm. "Wait—before you change, let me say this. That dress fits you like a dream. You made an excellent choice. We'll just need a couple of minor tweaks in the bodice to make it pop a little more, but other than that, it's perfect."

Tess smiles, her eyes misting over. "That means everything coming from you. You have no idea."

Tess holds onto my hand a moment longer. "You know... you and David have a lot in common. You both know how to listen, and you're both good at helping people talk through their mess with advice that actually makes sense."

I blink, caught off guard by the comparison and the way her words cling to me like perfume I didn't ask to wear.

"Would you like for me to give you his number?" she teases.

"Oh, no thank you. I'll pass," I say quickly, forcing a light laugh. But inside I'm wondering if the universe is trying to get cute with me.

After Tess leaves, I linger by the door, watching her walk away. Her posture's straight, her stride confident, but she's carrying a heavy load. There's always so much more going on under the surface than people let on. Her words play on repeat in my head: David stepped in, not just to fix contracts, but to smooth out the cracks in her and Amiri's relationship.

Maybe there's more to him than paperwork.

I sigh, finally turning away and heading toward the backroom, weaving through racks of veils and carefully boxed gowns. The energy in the workroom is different. Jasmine and Olivia huddle over a table, laughing softly as they sort through incoming orders.

"Did y'all know David was out here playing therapist for Tess and Amiri?" I ask, leaning on the counter with one eyebrow raised, breaking their conversation.

Jasmine pauses mid-laugh, looking up at me. "Wait, David Coleman?" she asks, her expression a mix of disbelief and amusement. "Mr. All About Me David?"

"Yup," I say, crossing my arms. "Apparently, he's more than just Mr. Contracts-and-Deadlines. Tess said he

74

talked her off the ledge when she almost called the wedding off."

Olivia smirks, tapping a pen against the stack of order sheets. "Man of many talents, huh? I'm surprised he didn't send them a contract and invoice for his intervention."

Jasmine chuckles, shaking her head. "So, what, he's just out here solving problems and mending relationships now? Who knew?"

"Trust me, I didn't," I mutter, grabbing a spare fabric swatch and running my fingers along the edges. "I thought he was just here to micromanage and make my life harder. But I guess... I don't know, maybe there's more to him than I thought."

Jasmine grins. "So, you're starting to think he's more than just a butthole?"

I roll my eyes, but I don't deny it. "Don't get it twisted. He's still a butthole. Just... a complicated one." I pause and think. "I guess it's just weird hearing about him actually caring about something other than rules and deadlines."

We all laugh, but even in my laughter, my mind is on the man I thought I had figured out. Maybe he's not just a walking clipboard with great hands and an annoying smirk. Or maybe I'm just reading too much into everything. Either way, I can't seem to get him out of my head.

That might be my downfall.

The last time I let a man occupy too much space in my thoughts, I ended up watching him walk away, leaving me with a broken heart and a stack of boxes to pack alone. I can't afford to lose focus again, especially not now when everything I've worked so hard for is finally happening.

David's the kind of man who could turn my perfectly structured world into chaos. I promised myself I'd never invite chaos back into my life again. At least, not on purpose.

Chapter Six

David

Loving You Was Complicated

The view from my office gives me a reason to smile every single day. The floor to ceiling windows alone are a flex that remind me how I built all this from the ground up. As I look out at the Atlanta skyline, I can only be reminded that focus, discipline, and control got me here. My office reflects my success with rich mahogany wood, modern décor, and not one thing out of place, just how I like it. Every inch of this space reflects who I am, or at least, who I've trained myself to be.

But something about today feels off.

"David? Are you listening?" Jacob Turner's voice slices through the speakerphone, pulling me back to the deal I'm supposed to be closing. A multi-million-dollar negotiation for Turner Enterprises, a company I've helped keep untouchable for years.

"Yes," I reply, sitting up straighter and flipping through the file in front of me. "You were saying something about the liability clauses?"

"Yes, I was. I was saying they need to be airtight," he says dryly, the irritation in his tone impossible to miss. "Which they're not, by the way. We need to revisit the language surrounding subcontractor responsibilities. Like I told you, I don't want any surprises on this. Our ducks have to be lined up in a row."

I nod out of habit, even though he can't see me. "Understood. I'll revise the language. Nothing will be left to chance."

"Are you sure? Is everything okay with you?"

"I'm good. I've got you."

"Good. The last thing I need is a lawsuit on my hands because of something we missed," Jacob says before launching into one of his infamous monologues about deadlines and contingencies. I've heard it all before, but today, his voice starts to fade into the background.

And that's when it happens.

Before I can stop it, Maya Thompson's face flashes in my mind, like an unwelcome but damn near impossible-to-ignore guest. In my thoughts, she's got her arms crossed, eyes sparking with fire, and her tongue ready to slice me in two. She has this way of looking at me that makes me feel like I'm the one being cross-examined.

Then, there are her thighs.

Lord. The woman's thighs are thick, strong, and unapologetic, like they've got their own gravitational pull. I can still see her standing across from me at the boutique, attitude reflected in her stance, daring me to step out of line. The image feels too vivid.

I shift in my chair and try to collect myself. Of all the things I should be thinking about like whatever in the hell Jacob Turner is grilling me about, it's Maya who's got my mind twisted in a knot. And the worst part of this is I can't even pretend that I don't love this feeling.

"Coleman?" Jacob's voice snaps me out of it, sharp and impatient.

"I'm here," I say quickly, forcing myself to focus as I flip through the contract in front of me. "We'll get the revisions done today."

"See that you do," Jacob groans before he ends the call without another word.

The line goes dead, but my thoughts are far from it. I drop the file onto my desk, exhaling sharply as I rub my temples. This isn't me. I don't get distracted. I don't let personal thoughts bleed into my professional life. Most importantly, I don't miss a beat.

Maya's got me all kinds of twisted. And I have no idea how to untangle my mind and get back in the game.

I lean back in my chair and stare out at the skyline, which is glass and steel wrapped in quiet chaos. Tess and

Amiri's contracts sit on my desk, reminding me of how I first got pulled into all of this.

About a month ago, I was the last one left in the office when Tess called in with a question. It wasn't about contracts or timelines. She needed clarity. Relationship clarity.

"David, be real with me... am I making a mistake?" Her voice was shaky, and not in a 'nervous bride' way. It was deeper than cold feet.

Her question stunned me. At first, I thought she was talking about the prenup. That was my lane, after all. Contracts, organization, and making sure people protected themselves were my lane. But this call wasn't about legalities.

"I don't have anyone else to talk to. I don't know what to do," she murmured. *"Lately, it just feels like... I'm on the outside of something I'm supposed to be in the center of. Like I'm showing up to my own life and someone else already has the lead role. We're not as close as we once were..."*

I can still hear the way her voice cracked, how her words came out in bursts between shaky breaths. She had called the office under the pretense of having questions about her prenup agreement, but in reality, she hadn't called our office looking to speak with a lawyer. She called because she wanted me to help her make sense of her relationship, which is a big task for a lawyer who knew nothing about her.

I remember sitting in this very chair, listening to her panic, and somehow finding the right words to pull her back from the edge.

"Since you're feeling all of these things, the best thing for you to do is talk to Amiri about your concerns," I say, my voice steady. "He chose you to be his future wife, and as a man, I know that's huge. It means you're someone he trusts to be by his side, so be honest with him, and I'm sure you guys will work this out."

She sighs on the other end. "It's just... sometimes I feel like I'm walking on eggshells. Like I have to be this picture-perfect fiancée. Everyone keeps saying we're goals, but inside, I'm freaking out."

I lean back in my chair. "You don't have to be perfect to be loved, Tess. You just have to be real. If you're afraid, say that. If you're unsure, say that too. A man who truly wants to build with you won't run from your honesty."

There's a pause. "But what if my honesty pushes him away?"

"Then that tells you everything you need to know," I reply. "But my guess is that it won't."

There's a long stretch of silence on the line before she breathes out like she's been holding it in for days. "You're good at this."

I chuckle. "Nah. I just listen. And I know what it's like to hold everything in until it eats you alive."

She goes quiet again. "I appreciate this, David. I know you're Lexington's company lawyer, so you represent Amiri's interest mainly, but when I met you to go over our prenup, I felt you were a good person. This conversation probably caught you off guard, but... thank you."

"You're welcome, Tess, but I'm here for both of you guys." I reply sincerely. "Just talk to him."

She called me back a week later and apologized for oversharing. She said things were getting better after they had a long talk. I told her I was glad I could help.

After that, I was invested in their future. I later talked to Amiri about how serious marriage is, and he told me he was committed to Tess and willing to do the work.

I feel good that they are in a good place, since their wedding is right around the corner. The contracts are ironclad, the planning is flawless, and their relationship seems untouchable again. It was because of my conversation with Tess that I felt obligated to make sure everything was perfect for her. Seeing Maya in the magazine and realizing her company was handling the wedding arrangements motivated me to dive in deeper to that obligation.

As I sit here now, I can't help but wonder why I'm so good at giving advice I can't follow myself. I told Tess to talk to Amiri and let him know how she feels. Yet I've yet to reach out to my ex and let her know how her walking out on me destroyed me for any other woman. All I've been doing is building walls, keeping everyone at arm's length, and letting people get close enough to see the surface but never the parts beneath. It's easier that way. It keeps me in control.

A knock at the door pulls me from my thoughts. I look up as Yolexis, my assistant, pokes her head inside.

Yolexis steps in with a thick stack of papers balanced in one hand and a fresh cup of coffee in the other. With her box braids swept up into a bun and a calm-but-commanding presence that somehow manages to check me without saying much, she's reminded me more than once that I forget to eat and drink when I'm buried in work. Today is one of those days.

"Mr. Turner's team finally sent over the revised documents," she says, setting the papers on my desk with a side eye glance. "Took them long enough. If you need me, I'll be at my desk, contemplating a career change that involves less chasing down incompetent attorneys."

I glance at the pile and smirk. "Appreciate you, Yolexis."

"Mm-hmm," she hums, already heading for the door. "Just don't make me have to *remind* you to review them before the deadline."

Classic Yolexis: efficient, quick witted, and always three steps ahead of me.

She flashes a quick smile and steps back out, leaving me alone with the contracts, the beautiful skyline, my wandering thoughts of Maya, and the haunting photo of Danielle that's still sitting face down on my bookshelf.

That damn photo. And all the other damn photos I've got of her at home, at the office, in frames that haven't moved an inch since she left with no warning or a real explanation. People don't get it, but when you don't get closure, it's like standing still while life demands you keep moving.

For three years, I've busted my ass. Passed the bar. Built one of the fastest-growing law firms in Atlanta from the ground up with my college buddy. And still, in the back of my mind and at the bottom of my soul, I held onto this twisted hope that Danielle would come back. That maybe—just maybe—we could put back all of the pieces together that shattered.

So, in a way, I guess those photos have been my anchors. They've been quiet reminders of the life I thought we'd build. Deep down, I know they're holding me in a place I should've outgrown. It's like when someone dies and they're forever the age they were at the time of their death. Right now, my love life is stuck on the day she walked out, and grieving lost love is a whole different kind of grief.

And then... there's Maya Thompson.

The way she looked at me when I stepped into her boutique. Like she saw right through the version of me I let the world believe. Like she wasn't impressed... but intrigued. She challenges me, matches my energy, and still somehow makes me want to be better.

Most importantly, I will never forget her thick, strong, and unapologetic thighs. Nah, those thighs live rent-free in my mind, and if they were charging rent to live in my mind, I would happily pay it. Honestly, I could write a damn book about them.

But it's not just that.

It's the way she doesn't flinch when she hears, *"David Coleman, corporate lawyer."* No tiptoeing. No fake smiles. She stands her ground, arms crossed, eyes locked on me like she knows I'm just a man who's still hung up on his first love.

I let out a long breath and try to shake her out of my head.

I'm attracted to her, but she's servicing one of my clients.

That's all this is.

Yeah, that's my story... and I'm sticking to it if I can.

The buzzing of my phone pulls me from my head. I glance at the screen, expecting to see Jacob Turner or another client's name flashing at me, but what I see instead stops me cold.

Danielle.

For a second, I just stare at the name glowing on the screen. My thumb hovers over the decline button, but something keeps me from pressing it. I let out a sharp breath and swipe to answer.

"Danielle," I say, my voice sounding detached.

"Hey," Her voice is soft, familiar in a way that feels like a gut punch. "How are you doing? It's been a while."

I can't believe she called me with a trivial 'how you doing' greeting like we're just two people who once knew each other from somewhere. I lean back in my chair and tighten my grip on the phone. "A while? Try years."

"You're right. It has been years," she parrots.

"Yeah, what's going on, Danielle? Why are you calling my phone?"

He hesitates before saying, "I'm back in town, and... I could use your help."

Danielle has always been able to bring me to my knees with a single request. Even now, my body reacts to the thought of her needing me. I'm already on my feet, pacing.

"You need help?" I ask with an edge to my voice. "What kind of help do you need?"

She exhales a shaky breath. "Times are rough right now, and I just need a place to stay for a few nights," she says. "I promise it won't be more than a week."

"A week?" I contemplate being in the same space as Danielle for a week, and none of the scenarios play out well in my mind.

She lets out another weary breath. "David, I don't know who else to call. Please..."

Gripping the phone tightly, I stop hearing what she's saying as my mind flashes back to the day she left. The day that I came home with all of her favorite things, only to find a Dear John letter that lacked an explanation, closure, or anything that would have allowed me to move on without feeling burned.

I'm sorry, but I can't do this anymore.

Please don't try to find me.

I need something different.

Forgive me.

—D.

All she left me were those words and an empty apartment.

Now, after saying she couldn't do it anymore, asking me not to find her, and saying she needs something different, three years later, she wants me to drop everything and help her like she didn't shatter my world.

"You can't just show up out of nowhere and expect me to drop everything," I say, my voice tense.

She pauses. "You're the only person I can trust. I don't know anyone else who would actually show up for me."

I close my eyes and pinch the bridge of my nose. A part of me wants to tell her no and remind her of how she left me, how she ripped the ground out from under me and walked away without looking back. But there's a small part of me, the part that still has that photo on my shelf, that can't completely shut her out.

Against my will, my voice is soft and considerate. "I don't know if this is a good idea, Danielle," I say, trying to talk myself out of doing what I know I'm about to do.

"I understand," she says quietly, but the disappointment bleeds through her voice. "I just thought I could stay with you for a few days, but... never mind. Forget I called."

"Wait." The word slips out before I can stop it. It hangs on the line as I try to figure out what the hell I'm doing. "Let me think about it."

She exhales, like she's been holding her breath. "Thank you, David. I'll text you the details, and if you decide to help me, I'll see you when you get here."

The line goes dead, and I set the phone down, staring at it like it's some kind of ticking bomb.

What is there to think about? Danielle isn't just any ex. She's *the* ex who broke me in a way no one else ever has.

Now, she's back, asking for help and stirring up emotions I tried to bury a long time ago.

The answer should be simple. I should've told her *hell no*. She spit on everything I was trying to build with her when she walked away without so much as a conversation. Buried somewhere in the mess of everything I'm feeling is that weak spot on my heart where Danielle left her imprint.

It's the same spot Maya's presence alone is finally starting to heal.

I sit back in my chair, my head spinning as I think about what I'm about to do...

And how easily it could dismantle my peace.

~*~

Later that evening, I'm behind the wheel, heading toward the Evergreen Hotel downtown. Danielle's text was simple with a location to pick her up, which is a request I've got no business honoring. Yet, here I am, gripping the steering wheel like it's the only thing keeping me grounded.

The hotel's sleek glass exterior glows under the streetlights as it comes in view. I pull into the circular drive and see her immediately. She's standing under the awning, one hand inside her tailored coat. Back in the day, Danielle always looked poised, polished, and unbothered, even in jeans and a t-shirt, and she still looks unbothered by the turmoil she left brewing inside of me.

She smiles when she spots me, and for a moment, just a moment, it feels like nothing's changed between us. It's like we're still in law school, laughing over late-night coffee runs and dreaming about the future. That moment passes quickly when I remember I'm no longer a student, no longer in love with her, and no longer the abandoned young man who didn't know what to do with himself.

I mentally lock every vulnerable part of me down, unwilling to let her see them again. She doesn't get to see what she meant to me. That privilege no longer belongs to her.

"David," she says warmly, like she's greeting an old friend.

I step out of the car and pop the trunk. "Get in," I say, my tone colder than I meant it to be. That's the only way I can speak to her right now without cracking. What else is there to say to the woman who shattered me? Do we small talk about the weather like she didn't gut me and walk away without glancing back? Do I ask her how life's been, like I actually want to know if some other man replaced me, used her up, and discarded her to this hotel?

Do I pretend I don't still carry her ghost around in pieces?

She nods and avoids my eyes as she wheels her suitcase to the trunk without another word. Suddenly, the silence between us grows louder than anything she could've said, and I'm okay with that.

Once she's settled in the passenger seat, I shut the trunk and slide back behind the wheel. I pull out of the driveway and into traffic, heading to my house.

The silence between us is filled with years of pain and unanswered questions.

Until she breaks it.

"Thank you for this. You didn't have to do it, but you came to help me," she says softly, and there's something in her voice that tells me she's been through hell.

I have no sympathy because she didn't have to go through hell. I would've taken care of her had she stayed with me. I would have made sure she never had to spend one night in a hotel with nowhere to go.

I grip the wheel tighter, my knuckles lightening from the pressure. "I'm still trying to figure out why I'm doing this."

She turns toward the window, her voice barely audible. "I deserve that."

There's a pause between us, filled with everything we never said.

"You know, a lot's changed over the past three years," she says finally.

I let out a cold chuckle. "No shit. I know a lot has changed."

Her breath catches. "You don't have to be rude. I know things didn't end the way either of us wanted, but I've followed your career. I'm proud of you."

I keep control of my emotions, especially the small part of me that still wants to believe in the version of us that actually believed in each other. "Yeah? Well, I lost track of you while I was busy building what we said we were going to build *together*."

"I didn't leave because I didn't love you," she says suddenly, and now her voice is shaking. "I left because I was scared."

The words land like a gut punch. They come at me like a combo from a UFC fighter, swift, brutal, and aimed straight for the weak spot. I clench my jaw and blink hard, fighting the flood of emotion that rises in my chest.

She was scared.

The kicker is we both were young and scared, but I chose to fight through my fear. I chose to make something happen for our future. I chose us.

Instead of fighting for us, choosing us... she left a note.

A note.

No conversation. No goodbye. No chance to fight for what we had.

She vanished and left me in our apartment like some half-finished project she no longer had time for. And now she wants me to believe it was fear?

My jaw ticks as I stare straight ahead, knowing good and well that I deserve an answer that's not wrapped up in vagueness and excuses. "Tell me what you were scared of? What type of fear could you have experienced that made you say fuck David?" The questions rush out of my mouth breaking the suffocating silence in the car.

She exhales slowly, her shoulders sinking like she's carrying a thousand secrets. "I know it seems like this was all about you. It wasn't. It was me. I wasn't strong enough for you, and for that I'm sorry. I was scared of everything, David," she says quietly, her voice trembling. "Of failing. Of losing myself in a relationship. Of... us."

"Us?" I shoot back in disbelief. "You were scared of us?"

She looks ashamed to admit it, but she does it with a nod of her head.

"Well, I have you to know you didn't just leave me. You left everything we built and had planned to build without so much as a conversation and with zero warning. Do you know what that did to me? Or did you care?"

"I cared. I—"

"I don't believe you cared! You couldn't have! People who care don't walk away from each other. They stay and talk it out. Even if you ended up leaving, you could have talked to me."

Her head snaps toward me. "Do you think it was easy for me to walk away?" she snaps, her voice gaining hostility. "Do you think I didn't agonize over it every damn day before I left? I didn't just wake up and say fuck David."

"Then why would you do it?" I demand. "Why leave? Why not talk to me? Why not let me in on the decision instead of shutting me out?"

She takes a shaky breath. Her fingers nervously toy with the strap of her purse. "Because I didn't know how to explain what I was feeling. You were so put together, so...

93

focused. You had everything mapped out from your career, your life, our future. While at the same time, I was drowning, losing myself in your world with each passing day. I pretended what you wanted was what I wanted, but I had actually lost touch with my true passion. There wasn't room for me to figure out who I was anymore."

I'm completely losing it now. I didn't think it was possible for me to grip the steering wheel any tighter, but I grip it so tightly that my knuckles ache. Her words cut deeper than I thought possible. "So, after pretending you wanted what I wanted, you just couldn't take it anymore, so you just up and left. You didn't trust me enough to be honest?" I say in a more measured and understanding tone. "If that's the case, we never had a chance, Danielle."

Her lip trembles, and she looks away, blinking rapidly as if she's trying to hold back tears. "I didn't think you'd understand. You have always been so sure of everything. I felt like I had to be just as sure, and I wasn't. I wasn't ready for all of it, and instead of talking to you, I ran away. I screwed up, okay? I know I hurt you. I just... I didn't know what else to do."

Her voice cracks at the end, and for the first time since this conversation started, I catch a glimpse of the woman I used to love. And it messes with me. It really does.

I shake my head, trying to make sense of everything she's saying. "You think I had it all figured out? Danielle, I was scared too. I was young and didn't have a clue of what I was doing, but I knew one thing: I wanted to do it with you. I wanted us to figure it out together."

She looks at me then, her eyes soft and glistening in the dim light. "I didn't know how to let you help me. I didn't know how to trust that you'd still want me if I admitted I didn't have it all together."

I laugh bitterly, the sound hollow even to my own ears. "So instead of trusting me, you left me. You made the decision for both of us. Do you have any idea what that did to me?"

She flinches at my words, but I don't stop.

"I spent years trying to understand what I did wrong, wondering what I missed, why I wasn't enough. Now, you're sitting here telling me you left because you were scared? Do you know how messed up that is?"

"I'm sorry," she whispers, her voice barely audible. "I know that doesn't fix anything, but I am. I'm sorry for everything."

I don't know what to do with her apology. Part of me wants to let it go, to just drive the rest of the way in silence. Another part of me needs more than an apology.

"Why show up after all these years? What do you really want from me, Danielle?"

She hesitates, her hands twisting in her lap again. "I don't know," she admits, her voice breaking. "I guess... I just wanted to see if there was still anything... if you could still—

" She cuts herself off, shaking her head. "Never mind. Forget I said anything."

I laugh, a short, humorless sound. "If I could still what? Trust you? Forgive you? Love you? What, Danielle? Say it."

She doesn't answer, her silence saying more than words ever could. As much as I want to press her and demand an answer, I can't bring myself to beg a woman for answers who walked away from me without so much as a well thought out Dear John letter.

"We're here," I say as I pull into my driveway.

I help her with her suitcase and show her to the guest room.

"David... I never stopped loving you."

I don't turn around. I can't. Instead, I grip the doorframe and reply, "Get some rest."

I retreat to my office, closing the door behind me and pouring myself a glass of bourbon. The first sip burns, but it's a welcomed distraction from the woman in my guestroom. She's got my mind messed up.

Danielle is the past, I remind myself. She's a chapter I closed a long time ago. The ending to that chapter cannot be rewritten.

I glance at the framed photo on the bookshelf, the one of me and Danielle at a dance years ago. It's still face down, but just knowing it's there is enough to cause tightness in my chest.

I let out a low groan, running a hand over my face. Danielle feels like a faded photograph. She's still familiar, but without the same vibrancy and spark as before.

I take another sip of bourbon, letting the warmth spread through me as I stare at the closed door. Danielle might be here now, but there's no erasing what she did. No erasing how she disregarded me.

I have to move on.

Chapter Seven

Maya

Miss Proactive Firecracker

I've been staring at the Lexington Enterprises contract all morning, highlighting sections, scribbling notes in the margins, and mentally prepping for the Brewster wedding chaos.

Jasmine, Olivia, and I have gone over every line to make sure it matches exactly what the bride and groom want. I already know David Coleman is going to find *something* to go on and on about. He always does.

I think about waiting for him to show up at the boutique unannounced with his clipboard in hand, ready to disrupt my peace and throw off my entire day with contract discussions. However, today, I decide to flip the script.

If he wants to nitpick every comma and dotted line, he's going to do it on *my* terms.

I smooth my blazer as the elevator doors slide open and I step into the sleek lobby of his high-rise kingdom.

The receptionist greets me with a polite smile as I approach. Her dreadlocks are twisted into a high bun, strands of copper, teal, and plum peeking through like a quiet rebellion. Everything else about her says polished and professional with her tailored blazer, glossy nude nails, and not a single sticky note out of place.

"Good afternoon. Do you have an appointment?"

"I'm here to see David Coleman. Tell him Maya Thompson is here with the Lexington Enterprises wedding contracts for the Brewsters," I say in a commanding, professional tone. But inside, my nerves are doing a little two-step.

Seconds from now, I'll be face to face with the man I spend too much time thinking about.

She nods and picks up the phone, speaking in low tones before saying, "He'll see you now. Just head down the hall to the last door on the left."

I stride down the hall toward his office. Every step I take, I feel a bit more anxious about seeing him again.

The moment I push open his door, I feel his presence before I even see him. He's seated behind a sleek glass desk, radiating that unbothered confidence that somehow manages to be both aggravating and... magnetic.

He looks up, his rich brown eyes locking on mine beneath perfectly arched brows, and for a second, I forget why I'm here. His cropped haircut is crisp like the rest of him. The man clearly pays attention to detail, and it shows. The afternoon light hits his medium brown skin and causes a glow that makes it real hard to focus on why I'm standing in his doorway.

"Maya, wow," he says, voice smooth like jazz vibrating through a late-night lounge. "I wasn't expecting to see you today. How'd I get so lucky?"

I ignore the slow smirk tugging at the corners of his lips and square my shoulders. I can't give that smirk any power. If I do, it'll take me down faster than I can blink. "We have a new Lexington client, and I figured it'd be easier to go through all this here," I say, walking further into his office and lifting the folder between us, "instead of you popping up at the boutique like clockwork."

He raises an eyebrow and leans back in his chair. "Hey, I thought you liked my visits. You don't like my visits?"

I roll my eyes. "Let's just say you popping up with contract issues during my creative time isn't exactly the highlight of my day."

He clutches his chest like I just stabbed him. "Your words wound me."

I laugh despite myself. "At least by coming here, I know you're actually in the zone of doing legal work."

His eyes lock with mine. For the briefest moment, they trail down to my thighs before he looks into my eyes again.

"Hmm." The sound is tremulous, like he's carefully considering his response. His tongue slowly and deliberately moves over his bottom lip, and then he bites down lightly, almost like he's trying to hold back a thought or tastes something invisible on his tongue. His gaze lingers a second too long, eating me up like I'm some kind of rare meal he's just discovered.

My body betrays me before I can stop it. Warmth spreads up my neck, and I shift from one foot to the other, suddenly feeling too seen. The tension between us is thick enough to cut with a knife, and I hate that my heart beats wildly simply from him looking at me.

"Well," he says, motioning for me to sit. "Let's take a look at what you've brought me."

I sit in the chair across from him and hand over the folder. His fingers barely briefly brush mine, but the contact shoots an unwanted tingle up my arm.

What in the entire hell.

Calm down.

You are not here for tingles and feels, Maya. You came to talk contracts, not to get thrown off your game by David Coleman and whatever hypnotic energy he's radiating today.

I remind myself of that fact, on repeat, but as David flips through the contracts, I'm hyper-focused on every move he makes. The way his brows furrow as he slips into lawyer mode. The way his jaw ticks when he spots something that needs revising. He's intense, meticulous... and so fine that it's distracting.

I drag my eyes away before I do something wild, like leap across his desk and kiss him like I've lost my mind.

My gaze wanders to the rest of the office. It's every bit as pristine and polished as the man behind the desk. Sleek furniture, abstract glass sculptures, file stacks so neat they look like they were measured with a ruler. The whole place oozes control, power, and precision.

One thing catches my eye that's out of place. It's a photo frame, turned face down on the bookshelf. The only imperfection in a room curated to perfection. Every other frame is upright, but this one is deliberately turned down. Now, I *really* want to know what's in that damn frame.

I can't help but wonder what memory or face he didn't want staring back at him every day. I'm curious, but I quickly turn my attention back to him before he notices me snooping.

"You've got a nice office," I say, still curious about the downturned photo.

He doesn't look up from the contracts. "Thanks."

"The pictures are a nice touch," I say, letting my eyes roam the office again. "Adds a little personality to all this...

lawyer perfection." I tilt my head toward the lone frame lying face down. "That one fall or something?"

His pen pauses mid-stroke. His eyes follow mine to the photo, and for a second, I catch the recognition and the break in his rhythm.

"No," he says quickly. He straightens in his chair, sets the pen down like it suddenly weighs too much. His jaw tightens, just slightly. "I just... haven't gotten around to fixing it."

My instincts kick in. There's a story behind that frame. One that has nothing to do with contracts or client meetings. I stand and step toward the bookshelf. "Want me to fix it?"

"No." His response is swift and final. "Don't worry about it."

"Hmm." I hum, tucking the reaction away like a secret for later. "Well, your decorator deserves a raise. This place is... intimidatingly nice. Like, I might get sued just for breathing wrong."

David's lips curve into a half-smile. "I'll be sure to pass that along." He gestures to the stack of papers between us. "Now, let's talk about these contracts you brought in. You've been busy. For this wedding, you're doing dresses for the bride, suits for the groom, and attire for the entire wedding party. You're also handling the ceremony and reception—totaling two hundred thousand dollars."

I nod, slide back into my seat, and cross my arms. "Exactly. That's why I pulled everything together and brought it in. I figured it'd be easier to run through it here than have you popping up at the boutique every other day."

The corner of his mouth twitches like he's fighting a grin. "Or maybe... you just wanted an excuse to stop by."

I narrow my eyes at him, refusing to let him get the upper hand. "You're cute, Coleman. Delusional, but cute."

He chuckles, low and warm, and it slides under my skin like silk over bare skin. "You keep calling me cute, Thompson. Might start thinking you've got a thing for me."

I roll my eyes, but my pulse is tap dancing in my throat. "Relax. That was a sympathy compliment. Don't let it go to your head."

David leans back in his chair, eyes never leaving mine. "Too late. Head's already gone."

I look away, pretending to study the edge of the desk like it holds the secrets to the universe. The truth is, this man is messing with my focus.

Not the contracts. Not the numbers. Him. His energy. His confidence. The way he looks at me like I'm not just the girl handling bridal orders but someone worth going to the moon and back.

Worst of all... some part of me wants to go to the moon. With him.

Before I know it, he is out of his seat and leaning casually against his desk in front of me. "For the record, you're not exactly hard on the eyes yourself."

My breath catches, but I quickly mask it with a raised brow. "Oh, is that your lawyerly way of saying you think I'm beautiful?"

"Beautiful," he repeats, his voice soft but deliberate, his eyes locked on mine like he's daring me to look away. "Doesn't quite do you justice, though."

I don't know why my heart's racing like this, but his words land square in my chest. I try to play it off like they don't affect me, but I'm losing that battle miserably. "So, what does me justice, Counselor?"

David's gaze drops for half a second, sweeping over me with an intensity that feels more like a caress than a glance. When his eyes meet mine again, there's no mistaking the heat behind them. "Stunning," he says finally, his voice barely above a whisper. "Bold. Captivating. Fine as hell."

"Look at you with your expansive vocabulary," I say teasingly.

"You bring out the big words in me," he fires back like he's been waiting for this moment. Then, his voice lowers slightly, like the next part isn't meant for anyone else to hear but me. "And I've gotta say... watching you work? Knowing you built something from the ground up, hold your own, stay graceful through what I know had to be hard times is more than impressive, Maya. It's rare. When you walk into a room, you don't just take up space, you shift it."

My stomach flips again, harder this time, and I can't think of a single smart-ass response. It feels good to hear him say what he sees when he sees me.

I tilt my head, trying to mask the way he's got my thoughts scattering like confetti. "You're not too bad yourself, Counsel. For a guy who shows up uninvited and nitpicks contracts like it's his life's mission."

That deep, warm laugh of his wraps around me like velvet and sends a shiver slowly down my spine.

"Somebody's gotta keep you on your toes, Firecracker," he says, eyes glinting with that smug lawyer charm.

I narrow my eyes. "Firecracker, huh? What makes you think you get to call me that?"

He steps closer with that lazy smirk tugging at the corners of his mouth. "Because every time I'm around you, something sparks. You light up the room... and damn near blow it up if you're in a mood."

I arch a brow, tilting my head. "Maybe you should be careful then. Firecrackers don't come with warnings."

He chuckles. "I like danger."

I roll my eyes, though the smile tugging at my lips betrays me. "Well, I like when we're not stuck going over contracts."

He leans in just enough to stir something under my skin. He's not close enough to touch, but enough to make my breath hitch. "You keep saying that... but I think you like it when I'm around."

I blink and slide right back into my rhythm. "Don't flatter yourself, Coleman."

"I don't need to flatter myself when you're already doing it for me, Thompson."

I should say something to shut him down, to put an end to this little game we're playing. But instead, I find myself sitting there, caught up in the motion, unable or maybe unwilling to pull away.

David watches me like he's peeling back layers I'm not ready to share. There's something about the way he looks at me, like he's trying to figure out what makes me tick, what's underneath all my walls. It's almost too much. Almost. But I hold steady, my arms crossed like a shield.

He clears his throat, straightens his tie, and glances at the contracts on his desk. "Alright," he says, his voice thick. "We should finalize these now."

I watch him walk back to his seat. "That's right," I say, crossing my arms tighter. "We're going to get everything straightened out today. So, if you've got something to revise, do it now."

He stares at me with a slight tilt to his head. "Let's get to work."

For the next hour, we review the contract line by line. He finds a few small adjustments, but mostly, everything's in perfect order. He's annoyingly thorough, but I can't lie to myself. There's something about the way his brain works, the way he homes in on details, that's... sexy. Not that I'd ever admit that out loud.

By the time we wrap up, my nerves are fried. Not because of the work, but because of his presence, his energy, and even his damn smirks. I gather my things and stand, squaring my shoulders. "So, are we good now? No more surprise pop-ins at the boutique?"

He leans back in his chair. "I wouldn't make any promises I can't keep, Firecracker. You seem to thrive under pressure."

I side eye him as I tuck the contracts into my bag. "I can handle the pressure. It's your timing that's the problem."

He stands as I turn to leave, and the movement catches me off guard. Suddenly, it feels like the room has shrunk and the walls are closing in. I clutch my bag tighter like it's going to save me from this... whatever this is.

As I reach for the door, I glance back to throw a parting jab, but when I spin around, he's right there, much closer than I expected. We're face to face, his gaze locked on mine, and all hell breaks loose in my mind, body, and soul like he just flipped the switch I've been trying desperately to keep off.

The teasing, the smart remarks, the push-and-pull all comes together in this moment. My breath hitches as I realize how close we are and how intoxicating it feels to be here. His scent, clean, sharp, and entirely too distracting, fills the space between us.

The space between us is barely there. I can feel his heat, his energy, the way his chest rises and falls with every breath. His eyes drop to my lips for a fraction of a second, so fast I almost miss it, but I don't. Oh, I don't.

David slowly leans in, causing my heart to pound so loud I'm sure he can hear it. "Maya," he murmurs, his voice so low that it does something to me.

I open my mouth to speak, but nothing comes out. My pulse is thundering in my ears, and for a second, I forget how to breathe. He doesn't move. Doesn't say a word. Just stands there with his mouth inches away from mine, watching me like he's daring me to make the first move. And I hate how much I want to. How much I want to lean up on my tiptoes, close the gap, and figure out what this tension would feel like if we let it snap.

But I don't.

I won't.

I back up two steps, force a smirk, and say the first thing that comes to mind. "See you around, Counselor."

I turn and walk out before I can let myself regret it. My heart is pounding, my hands are trembling, and I can feel his gaze on my back the whole way out. I hate how much I want to turn around. Hate how hard I will fold if I do.

I keep walking, clutching the contracts like they're some kind of lifeline. Because if I stop and give in to whatever this is, I'm pretty sure everyone in this office will know my name.

Whatever just happened in there can't happen again.

Chapter Eight

David

Playing Games

It takes everything in me to stop myself from going after Maya as she walks out of my office. I think about her for hours after she leaves. I think about her as I get in my car at the end of the day. I think about her as I stop to get gas after work and the whole drive home. By the time I enter my kitchen, I've already figured out what BS reason I will use to visit her boutique again.

It's Danielle standing in the middle of my kitchen like she belongs there that brings me out of my thoughts. She's barefoot, standing at the counter with her hair piled into a messy bun, pouring two glasses of E&J.

"It's the same whiskey we used to drink back in college when we didn't have the money but swore we were drinking the good stuff," she says, giving me a knowing smile. "Found this in the back of your liquor cabinet.

Thought it'd be fun to relive old times. Hope you don't mind."

My first thought is to tell her hell yes, I mind. That I don't do nostalgia. That the past should stay where it belongs—in the back of the liquor cabinet where she found it.

Instead of telling her those things, I shrug out of my suit jacket and loosen my tie. "I could use a drink."

She grins like she's already won something, sliding a glass toward me before pulling a board game from behind her.

Monopoly. Of course she wants to play Monopoly.

I shake my head, taking a slow sip of the whiskey. "Seriously?"

She eases over to the living room area and settles onto the floor where she's already set up the board. "Oh, come on, Mr. Big Shot Attorney. I know you remember our E&J and Monopoly days. Sit down and get ready to transport back to old times. Unless you're scared or something?"

I exhale, dragging a hand down my face and through my beard. "Scared? Nah. I ain't scared of shit," I say, letting the office vernacular go and bringing out my country grammar. "Let's not forget who ran when things got real." I kick off my shoes and sink to the floor across from her.

Danielle swirls the cheap whiskey in her glass, and her eyes lock with mine like she's searching for something that might still be there. "I deserve that," she says quietly as she sets her glass down with a loud clink. "Let's play."

The board game is easy. Familiar. The rhythm of it is like muscle memory, carrying me back to nights in a crammed dorm room where the biggest concern we had was stretching a bottle of this same cheap liquor through the weekend. I buy up real estate while she lands on Free Parking and celebrates like she just won the lottery. I shake my head, watching her throw her hands up in triumph, and something about the moment feels so damn simple.

We drink, we talk, we trade memories like currency.

She asks about my cases, my firm, and I tell her about the long nights, the courtroom wins, the empire I've built from the ground up. She listens, her chin propped in her hand, eyes gleaming with curiosity. Because the man sitting across from her is nothing like the one she left behind. She watches me like she's picking apart the differences and cataloging what's changed.

"The Governor's Ball is this weekend, right?"

I nod, taking a slow sip. "Yeah. How do you know about that?"

She shrugs, running a finger around the rim of her glass. "Saw the invitation on your shelf when I was looking for your board games."

I arch a brow. "You do a lot of looking around."

She smirks, tilting her head. "You have a nice home. Just getting acquainted with my surroundings."

I let that slide, setting my drink down. "Right."

She leans back against the couch. "So... you got a date to the ball?"

I pause, already knowing where this is going. "Haven't had time to think about it."

Danielle grins, stretching her legs out in front of her. "Well, lucky for you, I happen to be free that night." I shake my head, but she keeps going. "Think about it. We'd look damn good together. And hey, if you want me out of your hair or to 'find myself'—" she makes air quotes, "—what better place than a fancy event with a bunch of wealthy, successful men? Maybe one of them will be my knight in shining armor that will take me off your hands."

I exhale, rubbing my temple. "First of all, you're not on my hands or in my hair. We don't have any ties to each other, so let's get that understanding now."

Her voice cracks as she replies, "I—I understand that, David."

"Good," I say, returning to thoughts about the Governor's Ball. "As far as the ball, I hadn't planned to go because I don't have a date." I roll my glass between my palms. "It's not a big deal to me."

"It should be a big deal. It's an honor that you're invited to such an event."

I shrug. "Like I said, it doesn't matter if I go or not."

She leans forward, teasingly. "I clean up pretty damn well."

I chuckle, shaking my head. "Oh, I remember."

She smirks. "So, what do you say? You go to the ball with me as your plus one."

I should say no. Danielle in my space is like inviting in a storm and pretending I won't get wet. But what's the alternative? Skip the Governor's Ball? Miss out on one of the most prestigious nights of the year? Or worse—go alone and end up standing around looking like a lost man while my business partner shows up with his wife on his arm?

The thought crosses my mind to call Maya and ask her to come with me. She's the only one I want to take. The only one who would make walking into the ball with her on my arm feel like I've already won. With the way she pulled away from me in my office today after that damn near kiss that stopped time, I know better than to ask her.

She left like the room was on fire. She didn't look back. Didn't say a word. Just walked out, taking her radiating heat, her thighs, and beauty with her. The only sound louder than her heels on that polished floor was the silence she left behind.

I told myself it was just a moment. Just business. Just tension. But the truth was that silence felt personal. Like a door quietly closing. And if I reach out now, if I call her and she says no, I'm not sure I can pretend it doesn't sting.

So yeah... maybe letting Danielle be my plus-one makes sense.

It sure as hell doesn't feel right.

I take another sip of my drink and let the warmth settle in my chest. "Alright," I say finally, setting my glass down. "You can come as my plus one."

Her face brightens as she leans back with a smug little smile. "See? Accepting me as your date wasn't so hard."

Yeah. The hard part hasn't even started yet.

Because I know Maya's going to be at the ball.

Her boutique has been making waves. *Georgia Business Monthly* listed Dreamy Weddings as one of the most promising new Black-owned businesses in the state. Between that and the high-profile weddings she's planning, an invite to the Governor's Ball is practically guaranteed. Hell, she'll probably get a shoutout from the stage.

And I'll be standing there with Danielle, trying to act like my heart didn't damn near jump out of my chest when Maya walked into my office and almost kissed me.

I know one thing. If I step into that ballroom and see her wrapped around the arm of some overly moisturized finance bro with veneers and a pocket square, I'm going to lose my composure.

That'll be the hard part.

I can handle the press, the politics, the schmoozing. What I can't handle is seeing her laugh at another man's jokes. What'll wreck me is knowing I hesitated and somebody else didn't.

As we wrap up the game, the tension between Danielle and me shifts into something mellower. She picks up the empty bottle of E&J and turns it in her hand, a half-smile tugging at her lips.

"Crazy how things change," she says. "Back then, this felt like luxury."

I chuckle, allowing myself to remember some of the good times we shared. "We were so bright-eyed and bushy-tailed back then. Everything felt like luxury, the cheap drinks, free pizza, study nights that turned into sleepovers." I swirl the liquor in my glass and take a slow sip, letting the burn settle in my chest. "But things change," I add, quieter this time.

Danielle glances at me over the rim of her glass, her eyes lingering like she's searching for something in my face. Then she rises slowly, stretching like she used to after long nights curled up on my couch. She arches her back with her hands deliberately overhead. She knows what she's doing. Knows I used to trip over my feet to get to her when she arched like that.

"Well," she murmurs, setting her empty glass on the table, "they say the more things change, the more they stay the same."

Her tone is soft, a little smoky, suggestive in a way that reminds me of late nights and heated kisses.

"Thanks for letting me stay, David. Really. I'm headed to bed."

I nod, eyes on the drink in my hand instead of the curve of her hip as she walks past me. "No problem."

She walks past me with a sway that's anything but innocent. Her fingertips graze my shoulder as she leans in close, just enough for her breath to brush my ear. "You don't have to sleep alone tonight," she whispers. "It's your house. You can sleep in whatever bed you'd like."

Heat radiates from her skin. Her words linger and try their best to sizzle in my spirit. I can feel the warmth tugging at the familiarity rooted deep in my chest and moving lower.

Danielle's never been subtle. She's always taken what she wanted. It's clear she wants to remind me of every night we used to spend tangled in sheets and passion.

She steps away slowly, sending one final look over her shoulder as she disappears down the hall, her hips swaying with intent.

She thinks I will follow her, make love to her, and sink so deeply into her that I will forget who I am again... who she made me become.

I stay rooted to my spot on the floor.

What I want isn't in that room. It's probably working late in a boutique across town, with mocha skin, fire in her voice, and a name I haven't stopped thinking about since the moment she said it.

Maya.

My Firecracker.

What I wouldn't give for her to be walking down my hallway after an invitation to join her in bed.

Chapter Nine

Maya

The Governor's Ball

I tried real hard to forget about the Governor's Ball. Would've much rather been curled up on my couch with a glass of wine, flipping through craft magazines, figuring out new ways to bling out wedding shoes or bedazzle a clutch that'll make a bride cry happy tears.

But Olivia and Jasmine weren't having it. They made sure I remembered the importance of attending the ball, which is why I'm standing in my bedroom, arms crossed, staring at the plum gown laid across my bed.

We've been invited to rub elbows with Georgia's elite. The movers, the shakers, the check-writers will be out in full force tonight. This is our moment. Time to step out, show out, and let these people know Dreamy Weddings isn't just some cute trend... it's couture and here to stay.

My phone dings with a message from Olivia, who's been ready and waiting for this event for weeks. She sent me a picture thirty minutes ago of her standing in front of her mirror wearing a flowing bronze gown and her hair flat ironed to perfection.

Olivia: Are you ready to go...or?

Me: Uh...give me a few minutes.

Olivia: Okay. Jas and I are on the way to get you.

Me: Okay.

I exhale, tossing my phone onto the bed beside my dress.

Back when my ex couldn't begin to understand how badly I wanted to be a designer, I used to dream of moments like this; moments where people would recognize my work, where I'd walk into a room and know I belonged because I created something worth noticing. Troy used to entertain my ideas, smile through my talk about fabrics and sketches, even encouraged me... as long as it stayed a hobby. He never saw the vision. Never saw *me* as someone who could own a creditable and profitable business.

To him, I was just a girl with a Pinterest board and a side hustle fantasy.

And that hurt...

But look at me now.

I've made it. I'm one of Georgia's rising businesswomen, invited to the Governor's Ball, and I'll be dressed in a gown from my own boutique. Those aren't the moves of someone with a hobby. That's history in the making.

For a second, I wish Troy could see me now.

Then I laugh softly to myself.

He doesn't deserve to see me now. That would mean he would have to be in the room, and he doesn't deserve to be in the same rooms I worked to be in. Especially, since he chose to leave me when it was all a dream.

I shake off the trip down memory lane, grab my dress, and run down a list of affirmations. "I worked for this. I pushed through the doubt, the pressure, the people who couldn't see the vision and made this dream my bitch. I deserve to be in this moment, standing tall at a ball with the Governor."

There's a knock at the door, and when I answer it, Jasmine steps in looking flawless.

"Girl, why aren't you dressed? You better not be in here doubting yourself," Jasmine calls out as she steps in, a soft smirk playing on her lips. "You're about to shut this whole place down, so let's get some pep in your step. We're waiting on you."

She follows me down my hallway as I head to my room, my dress still laid out on the bed. "You look good," I tell her, giving her the once-over and meaning every word.

Jasmine's rocking a deep emerald green velvet gown that hugs her curves like it was sewn on. The high slit in the front gives just the right amount of leg, and the plunging neckline is tasteful but bold—very her. Her locs are swept up into a crown-like bun, a few pieces curled and hanging down to frame her face just right. Gold statement earrings catch the light as she turns her head and smirks at me.

"You better not outshine me," she teases, tossing a look over her shoulder.

"Please, I'm just going for the photos and the champagne," I assure her.

Jasmine walks over and picks the dress up off the bed. "That makes two of us. Now, let's get you dressed, so we can get this show on the road."

A few minutes later, Olivia strolls into my room like she's stepping onto a runway.

"Whew, okay Liv," I say, letting out a low whistle. "You look like money dipped in magic."

Her shimmering bronze gown catches the light with every move. Off-the-shoulder, form-fitting, and dramatic in all the best ways, the dress trails behind her just enough to make a statement without doing the most. Her hair is bone-straight and tucked behind one ear to show off a diamond ear cuff that sparkles every time she tilts her head. Her face is beat to perfection with arched brows, highlighted cheekbones and rich mocha lip gloss.

Olivia twirls and smirks. "I told y'all I wasn't showing up looking like that girl who work at the boutique. Tonight, I'm a CE-to-the-O."

"As you most definitely are!" I grin, giving her a once-over. "Both of y'all look like y'all came dipped in luxury."

"And we are," Jasmine adds, flipping her hair. "You too, boo!"

Olivia laughs. "Okay, okay. Are we ready to shut this thing down or what?"

I grab my clutch. "Let's do it."

We head out and pull up to Azalea Cove Resort like a Black girl dream team.

The moment we step inside the resort's ballroom, it's like walking into another world. In this world aged wine and expensive champagne flows like water, designer labels glide across marble floors, and the air is thick with money, power, and ambition.

I barely get two steps inside before I feel an undeniable shift in the atmosphere. It's the kind of energy that crawls across my skin. My chest tightens before I even know why.

Something... or someone... is doing this to me. I can only think of one person who has been making me feel this way.

Oh, my God. He's here.

I should have known he would be here. How could I not have known?

I do my best to ignore the way my body is responding to just the thought of him being here. My skin's buzzing like it knows something I don't. I glance around the ballroom, admiring the tall ceilings, golden chandeliers, and the sea of people draped in money and influence. When I don't spot who I'm searching for, I chalk the feeling in my gut up to nerves and remind myself that I'm single and here to mingle.

A waiter passes by with a tray of champagne, and I grab a glass, lifting it to my lips. The tiny bit of alcohol in the champagne is not working fast enough to calm my nerves as my eyes sweep the room.

Then, I see him.

David Coleman.

He's the reason I've felt this way since the moment I walked into this ballroom.

I should look away and pretend he's just another face in the crowd, but my eyes betray me. They stay locked on him, drinking in all six-foot-something of him. He's wrapped in a black tux that fits him *too* well like he and the suit were built for moments like this.

In a way, it feels like a cruel trick to be so attracted to him.

Especially since he's here with a date.

I wish his looks were the only thing that had me in a chokehold. The other thing is the woman standing next to him, draped in gold, smiling like she was made to fit right at his side. The way her body angles toward his and things like the subtle brush of his arm against hers tells me everything I don't want to know about them.

Confusion startles me momentarily, but I quickly recover. I could've sworn something was building between us. Sworn that if I had leaned in just one inch closer that day in his office, our lips would've met in the kind of kiss people write poetry about.

Staring at his lips now, I realize if I *had* kissed him, it would've been a mistake. More importantly, it would have been a betrayal, not just of my pride, but of the woman at his side.

I shake the thought loose and force my face to stay neutral.

Don't show how you feel... don't show how you feel, Maya, I chant to myself.

A couple of champagne gulps helps me swallow the lump in my throat and train my features into something that doesn't scream *heartbroken.*

"Maya, are you even listening?" Olivia nudges me, pulling me out of my head.

"Hm?" I blink, forcing my attention back to her and Jasmine.

Olivia follows my gaze, and when she sees what—or who—I'm looking at, her lips curve into a knowing smirk. "Well, damn. That's a plot twist."

I roll my eyes. "It's not a plot. It's just David. With a date. Not my business."

Jasmine arches a brow. "You sure about that?"

"Positive."

It's a lie, and we all know it, but I refuse to let it matter. I'm a boss. A powerhouse. A woman who left heartbreak in the past where it belongs.

And David Coleman is *not* the exception.

So, I do what I do best. I straighten my shoulders, flash a winning smile, and prepare to work the room like I was born for this. "Let's mingle."

Jasmine tilts her champagne glass. "Lets!"

We move through the crowd, shaking hands and making connections. All the while, that attraction to David and awareness that he is near never goes away. Several times, I glance across the ballroom, and our eyes lock, and suddenly, I can't breathe.

Jasmine and Olivia flank my sides, looking good and feeling good. My plum-colored number hugs my curves in all the right places with the high slit giving just enough to be tasteful but flirty.

After seeing David over there with *her,* I do feel off kilter tonight. Like I could latch on to some powerful man and become whatever he wants me to be for one night. Just so I can get over the feeling I feel right now.

But that's so not me.

I'm here for business, networking, and rubbing elbows with potential clients. So, that's what I'm going to do. I'm not going to continue to give in to the familiar tug that draws my attention across the room.

It doesn't matter that he's standing near the bar, looking like a chocolate king in an all-black tux. Or that his hair and beard are neat and shiny. He's polished from head to toe like he walked straight out of a luxury magazine. His signature confidence is on display, commanding the space without trying. Yeah, none of that matters.

The woman beside him leans in slightly as she says something that makes him smirk.

I hate that stupid-looking, sexy ass smirk. I hate that it still does something to me, even though another woman is making him do it. I straighten my shoulders, pasting on the expression I've mastered, which includes a blend of unbothered, confident, and untouchable.

I push my focus back to the event. I have work to do, which includes networking, shaking hands, securing future business for Dreamy Weddings.

David Coleman and his date don't factor into that.

At least, that's what I keep telling myself.

"Whew, girl," Olivia murmurs beside me, sipping her champagne like it's tea. "That man over by the grand piano been watching you like you built the building."

"Which one?" I ask, scanning the room quickly, half-hoping she means David and half-hoping she doesn't.

"The one in the navy suit with the salt-and-pepper beard," Jasmine answers, grinning. "He looks like he owns three banks and a yacht in Barbados."

"I'll take the yacht," I say, smirking. "And the bank accounts."

We all laugh, and for a moment, I let myself relax, floating through conversations with donors, judges, influencers, and a few folks from city council. We pass out business cards, take selfies, and drop enough flirtatious smiles to make any high-end marketing firm proud.

Just as I'm starting to feel back in my element, a poised woman in a floor-length gold gown steps up to us with a megawatt smile. She's all elegance and confidence, her energy commanding but warm.

"You must be the ladies behind Dreamy Weddings," she says, extending her hand. "I'm Brielle Williams. My husband's law firm works closely with Lexington, and I've heard *so* much about your boutique from our clients."

"Oh wow," Olivia says, shaking her hand first. "Thank you! That means a lot."

"I've seen your work. Stunning. The Atlanta area needed a Black-owned bridal boutique with your level of luxury. Putting it in the suburban area of Azalea Cove was brilliant. I've been telling everyone to check y'all out."

My cheeks warm. "That means everything coming from you. Thank you so much."

"Ladies, meet my husband, Will," she says, motioning behind her. A tall man with broad shoulders and a charming smile approaches, dressed in a custom tux that screams old money and long hours at the firm.

He shakes our hands politely before turning to someone just behind him. "And here comes David—my partner."

Time stops. Just a little.

Because, of course, David Coleman would walk up right now with that same energy that makes me forget how to function. And let's not forget the woman on his arm.

Her arm is looped through his like it belongs there. Her dress is gold and shimmery, matching Brielle's, and her smile is a little too wide.

"Ladies, this is David Coleman," Will says, oblivious to the fact that my soul just tried to leap out of my body. "And this is his guest, Danielle."

David's eyes meet mine and hold. For one second. Two. Long enough to light a match inside me and blow it out just as fast.

"Nice to meet you," Danielle says, her voice syrupy sweet as she extends her hand to me.

I shake it politely. "Maya Thompson."

"Oh," she says, cocking her head slightly, like she recognizes the name from somewhere. "I've heard of you."

David clears his throat, his gaze flicking to mine again before quickly shifting to Will. "Excuse us, just for a second."

He pulls Will aside, talking business, but I catch him glancing back at me more than once. Jasmine and Olivia exchange a glance but say nothing.

The second he walks away, I finally breathe again. I feel a temporary release from the chokehold he's had on my senses since I stepped into this ballroom. Seeing him with Danielle is like swallowing fire with a smile on my face. I don't know why it bothers me this much. We're not anything. Not really.

That didn't stop me from feeling every inch of her body pressed into his side like she has a claim to him.

Danielle turns to me. "Love your dress. It's bold."

I smile, the one I reserve for women who think they've won something. "Thank you. I designed it."

"Oh... wow." Her smile fades for half a second. "That's... impressive."

"Thank you," I say again, my voice calm and collected. "It's what I do."

"We're definitely going to have to get together soon, ladies," Brielle says before she moves on to speak to a popular influencer.

Jasmine leans over, whispering, "You okay?"

I nod, sipping my champagne. "I'm fine."

That's a lie.

I'm still trying to process the heat in David's eyes when we locked gazes a few minutes ago. That wasn't casual. That wasn't friendly. That was a man looking at a woman like he's trying to remember every inch of her.

And yet, he's here with her.

David returns with his smooth confidence. His suit hugs him perfectly, and his intense eyes are trained right on me, and not Danielle.

His attention lingers far too long on my dress and the slit along my thighs. "Plum, huh?" he says, his voice low. "Didn't think I could like that color more than I do right now."

My pulse skips. "I like your suit. You've got good taste."

"I do," he says without missing a beat. "Thank you."

Our eyes lock. And for a moment, the noise fades. The clinking glasses, distant music, and laughter all dims until it's just us in a tense, electrified silence.

Danielle clears her throat and steps closer to him, looping her arm through his again. "I'm hungry," she says, her voice tight. "Let's go make a plate before all the good food's gone."

David doesn't look at her. He keeps his eyes on me.

I try to hold my ground, but his stare has gravity. It's like he's being dragged into an orbit and is working to pull me in with him. Sad part, he doesn't care who's watching.

"I'll catch up with you," he murmurs without moving.

Danielle stiffens beside him, her lips tightening. "Okay," she says, unable to hold the fake smile any longer. She walks off toward the food bar.

He waits until she's out of earshot, then shifts closer to me. Not close enough for anyone to call it disrespectful, but close enough that I can feel the heat coming off him. Close enough that I can smell the faint scent of spice and something warm and clean.

Everyone else continues talking, while we drift off to our own conversation.

"I had started to think I wouldn't see you here tonight. Imagine my face when you walked in..." he says.

"I imagine you didn't miss a beat. You get invited to events like this all the time, right?" I keep my tone light even though my heart is sprinting.

"Ever since I landed my first big client a year after finishing law school, I have been invited here," he says, "but tonight... tonight I was hoping I'd run into you."

I raise an eyebrow. "With your date on your arm?"

"She's not my date-date," he says smoothly. "She's just... an old friend."

I blink. "And I'm what? A new friend?"

His mouth curves into a knowing smile. "You're the reason I can't sleep. The reason I came tonight dressed like

I might run into the woman who flipped my world inside out without even trying."

My mouth opens slightly, but no words come out.

He takes one small step closer. "Let me be real with you, Firecracker. You can pretend you're unaffected by what's been happening between us, but I see it. I feel it. Same way I know you feel it too."

I lick my lips before I can stop myself. "This is not the time or the place to talk about this. You're here with a date."

"I don't care." His voice drops. "I'd say it on the damn stage with the governor listening if I had to."

"Don't," I whisper. "You don't get to say things like that when you're showing up with someone else."

"I know," he says quietly. "I know it's messy. But so is wanting someone you can't stop thinking about... and realizing she's the only person in this room who actually sees you."

He's not lying. I see him. I've seen him since the first time he strolled into my boutique with that smug look and a clipboard full of expectations, acting like his suits gave him authority over me. I saw past his title and arrogance and straight into the man.

And that's the problem.

"Enjoy your night, David," I say, trying to keep my voice even. "I'm sure we'll meet again... to discuss contracts."

It's a weak shield, and we both know it. But it's the only one I have to shield my heart right now.

I take a step back.

He takes one forward.

His dark eyes search mine, slow and intense, asking questions I've spent weeks dodging.

What are we doing? Why do you run every time it feels real? What would happen if we stopped pretending this doesn't mean something?

I don't have answers. Not ones I'm ready to say out loud. But my silence doesn't stop him.

He leans in, and everything around us fades. The soft jazz, clinking glasses, laughter, and the chatter of Georgia's elite all go away. All I can feel is the warmth rolling off his skin and the way my chest tightens in the intensity of the moment. His lips are so close, all he'd have to do is tilt forward and—

"Don't," I whisper, so faint it barely leaves my lips.

His brows twitch in a flash of confusion or maybe hurt. "Maya—"

"I can't," I say, this time clearer. "Not here. Not like this."

I see the restraint in his jaw, the way his hands clench at his sides like he's trying to stop himself from gripping every part of me.

I shake my head, tearing myself out of the haze. My heels click against the marble like an escape plan. I don't look back. I can't. If I do, I know I'll run to him instead of away.

I clutch my champagne like it might hold me together.

For the rest of the night, I feel his eyes on me as I move through the room, through conversation after conversation. Maybe it's my imagination, but every time I laugh, I wonder if he hears it. Every time someone says my name, I wonder if he tenses.

Of course, my thoughts are insane.

He's not thinking of me. He's with her. And she's beautiful, elegant, poised. She knows exactly when to touch his arm, exactly when to smile for the camera, and exactly how to show the world he's hers.

Good for her.

I don't care.

I don't.

After a full hour of whispering that lie to myself like a chant, I prove it. When a tall, smooth-talking brother in a tux that fits like it was sewn by the gods offers me a hand and a smile that could melt ice, I take it.

And for three minutes, I dance like I've never been watched.

Even though I know I am.

Chapter Ten

David

What is She Doing?

I swirl the last sip of bourbon in my glass, but my focus isn't on the drink. It's on my Firecracker.

I wasn't thinking when I invited Danielle as my plus one. I knew Maya would be here. She's a big deal in Azalea Cove, and her influence as a wedding planner stretches out to the surrounding cities. Her Atlanta client base is huge, making Dreamy Weddings a go-to boutique for the city. Of course she'd be at an event the governor was adamant on hosting here to highlight Azalea Cove's growth and potential.

But knowing it and seeing her are two different things entirely.

She walked into the ballroom like the floor was built just to feel her heels. That plum-colored gown hugs every inch of her like it was sewn onto her skin. That slit... God, that slit. The way her thighs moves through it with each step is damn near criminal.

It's not just her body that has me locked in place. It's her presence. That fire in her eyes that doesn't dim, not even under these chandeliers or in a room full of millionaires and politicians. She belongs here. She owns this space. And I can't look away—neither can any other man in here on the brink of getting his ass kicked for looking at what's mine.

Danielle is talking beside me, but her words sound like wind. All I hear is the click of Maya's heels, all I see is her smile as she works the room with Jasmine and Olivia. I know she feels me watching her. She straightens her shoulders every time our eyes meet across the room.

I take that final sip of bourbon and let it burn my chest. I wish like hell I could walk away from Danielle and toward Maya without setting the entire night on fire. But damn it, I'm willing to let it all burn for her.

She's been in my line of sight all night like gravity, pulling my focus no matter how many people I talk to or how many times Danielle tries to loop her arm through mine.

Then, I see red.

Maya's decided to let the night burn. She's on the dance floor, wrapped in the arms of some smooth-moving, dark-skinned brother in a sharp tux with that cocky, confident posture. His hand's are low on her back, and I mean, way too low. They're right at the curve of her hip, and he's moving with that kind of rhythm that can make another man jealous on instinct alone.

He's saying something in her ear, and she's laughing like she's got no worries in the world and like she didn't just nearly kiss me a couple hours ago. Like I haven't been standing here wondering how the hell I'm supposed to act like I'm not coming undone at the sight of her.

Then, I hear Danielle's voice beside me. "Do you want to dance?"

I look at her like I don't understand why she's here. There was a time I would've killed to be asked that by her. A time when her hand reaching for mine meant something. When being next to her made sense. Now, it's like trying to force a puzzle piece that doesn't fit.

Glancing back at Maya, I see her body swaying and lips parted in a smile I want to be the cause of. I offer Danielle the softest shake of my head. "Not tonight."

Her glow falls apart before she looks away, pretending it doesn't matter.

Shifting my attention to Maya, I watch as she leans closer to that man on the dance floor. A surge of jealousy runs through me so hot I damn near forget where I am. While I'm stuck here, playing nice with a woman who stopped seeing me years ago, the one who does is dancing with someone else.

Suddenly, it feels like somebody cut off the air in the room because I can't fucking breathe.

I grip my glass tighter than tight, my smirk gone, my jaw clenching as something dark shifts through my chest. It's unfamiliar but impossible to ignore. What in the world is happening to me? This feels worse than the day I came home to find Danielle gone from our apartment years ago.

Danielle perceptively follows my gaze. "You good?" she asks, stirring her drink lazily.

I don't respond right away. Instead, I watch as Maya leans in, letting the man whisper something against her ear. Her smile is wide, her body moving effortlessly in rhythm with his.

Something inside me *burns*. I mean, it really burns.

"I'm fine," I lie to Daneille and throw back the rest of my drink. My grip on the empty glass is too tight, so I carefully set it down. If I don't, I might just crush it in my hand.

Danielle lets out a soft laugh. "You sure about that?"

I don't answer. I'm already moving.

The man twirls Maya, spinning her with ease. When she lands against his chest, laughter spills from her lips, and I feel something inside me crack wide open.

I've had enough of this.

As I move through the crowd, I'm barely aware of the conversations happening around me. I don't care how this looks. I don't care that Danielle is watching me with amusement laced in her expression. I don't care that Maya looks like she's having the time of her life.

All I know is I need to stop this.

I step onto the dance floor without hesitation, cutting into their space like I belong there. The man barely gets a chance to react before I speak.

"Can I cut in?"

The way I'm looking at him like I'll split his head down the middle if he gives me a reason makes it clear it's not really a question. I'm not here to negotiate. I'm claiming her.

"That's up to the lady," he says, glancing at Maya for her response.

She tilts her head, those dark eyes locking with mine like she's deciding whether to slap me or kiss me. "Interesting that you want to dance now that I'm already dancing with someone," she says coolly. "How will your date feel about this?"

I don't blink. "I'm a single man. I can dance with whomever I like."

"And so can I," she fires back, gesturing between her and her current dance partner.

I step closer. "But I want to dance with you."

Her lips part, just slightly. She hesitates, looking at me like she wants to say more but can't find the words. That hesitation tells me everything I need to know.

The guy chuckles, stepping back with a good-natured shrug. "She's all yours, man."

I already knew that.

The second he steps back, I take his place, pulling Maya's body flush against mine, my hand pressing against the small of her back. She fits perfectly just like I knew she would.

Her breath hitches, just slightly, before she catches herself, tilting her chin up like she's daring me to make a move.

I lean in, my lips brushing close to her ear.

"You like making me upset."

She scoffs, but the way her body reacts tells me a different story. "Why would you be upset that I'm dancing with someone? You have an entire *date*, David."

"It's not like that."

"Oh really?" she counters, her voice dripping with disbelief. "Then tell me... how is it?"

I don't answer. Instead, I move us in a slow, deliberate sway, keeping her locked in place against me.

But Maya isn't easily swayed.

She pulls back just enough to meet my eyes. "You know what? Never mind. We're not dating. Why are we even having this conversation?"

I don't respond. Instead, I take her hand and *lead* her off the dance floor, weaving us through the crowd until we step outside onto the dimly lit balcony. The air is cooler out here, a sharp contrast to the heat simmering between us.

Maya pulls her hand from mine and crosses her arms. "So, this is what we're doing now? Dragging people off the dance floor when we don't like what we see?"

I step closer, lowering my voice. "Okay, so it's true. I didn't like seeing you with him."

She lets out a breathy laugh, shaking her head. "So, first of all, we're not dating, so it shouldn't matter to you who I dance with. Let me also remind you again that you're here with another woman."

"Maybe it sounds crazy, but I brought her here as a plus one, not as a date. We're not together. She's an old friend accompanying me here. She can leave here with another man tonight and it wouldn't bother me one bit. You, on the other hand..."

She searches my eyes for the rest of my statement, but the tension between us speaks for itself. It's electric and damn sure *undeniable*.

Then, she moves... or maybe I do.

It doesn't matter.

One second, we're standing inches apart, trading heated words, and the next I've got one hand gripping the curve of her waist, the other sliding up to cradle the back of her neck as I crush my mouth to hers.

Maya's gasp enters my soul, implanting itself there. It's not the sound of protest. It's the sound of need. Her

147

fingers fist into the lapels of my jacket like she's ready to hold on forever. She pulls me so close that I can feel every curve of her body pressed to mine. Every breath she takes vibrates through me.

Just like that, the fire we've been ignoring for too damn long ignites into a full-blown inferno.

I kiss her like I've wanted to from the moment I laid eyes on her. The kiss is deep and slow. I drink from her lips like I'm starving. Her lips are soft, warm, and when her mouth opens for me, I lose all grip on where we are or who might be watching.

When she moans, the sound dismantles me, taking me apart one piece at a time.

My hand slips lower, pulling her closer, pressing her body against mine until there's no space left between us. She tastes like champagne and trouble, and I'm more than ready to drown in both.

She shifts, and her luscious thighs brush mine in all of their thickness. They are finally where they belong, pressed against me. Now that I've got both of them in my possession, I've got plans. Big ones.

Her leg slides between mine as we press into the cold railing of the balcony. I don't care that the music's thumping behind us or that voices drift just a few feet away. All I care about is the woman in my arms, and the fact that right now, she's kissing me like she's just as gone.

My mouth leaves hers, trailing kisses down her jaw, grazing the spot just below her ear that makes her shiver. "Maya," I whisper, voice thick with need, "I want you."

She gasps, her breath hitching. She curls her fingers around the back of my neck, pulling me in again, her mouth finding mine like she can't get enough.

And God help me, I can't either.

Her hands slide under my jacket, fingertips skating along my back like she's memorizing me. My lips find her throat, and her head tips back, offering herself up like she's mine already.

"Shit," she breathes, suddenly tensing beneath my hands. She pulls back, eyes wide and lips kiss-bruised. Her chest rises and falls fast like she just ran a marathon. "We're outside," she says, voice shaky. "We're literally outside the Governor's Ball making out."

Reality hits me in the gut. "Yeah," I breathe, stepping back, running a hand over my face.

"We were about to—"

"I know."

She looks at me like she can't believe she lost control of the moment. "I almost let you... out here where people are close by," she whispers, shaking her head. "You make me lose my damn mind."

I reach for her again, gentler this time, resting my hands on her hips. "No... I make you feel. And I don't apologize for that."

149

She looks torn between wanting to run and wanting more. "I have to go back in," she says, looking as if she's still breathless, still burning. "Yeah, let me go back in before I forget who I am again."

"Come home with me," I say before I can stop myself.

She stares before leaning in and pressing a kiss on my cheek. "Not tonight," she whispers, then pulls back to look into my eyes. "Maybe next time we should try a date before you have me pinned against a balcony wall and then take me home."

"You're right. I'll take you on as many dates as you want to go on."

She smirks that signature Maya smirk that's equal parts challenge and charm. She smooths her hands down the front of her dress and reclaims her composure. "Talk to you soon then," she says, turning to walk inside with the kind of sway in her hips that tells me she knows exactly what she's doing and exactly what she's making me wait for.

I'm left standing here, heart racing, jaw clenched, and already planning the best damn date she's ever had.

Chapter Eleven

Maya

This is Crazy

I step back into the ballroom like I didn't just almost let a man unzip both my soul and my dress out on that balcony, a few feet from every power player in Georgia. My hand smooths down the front of my gown, like I can press the chaos back into place, like I didn't just lose my whole mind—and nearly my dignity—on the balcony.

I can still feel the way his body responded to mine. The press of him against me, the heat lingering in his kiss, and the soft sound that escaped when I kissed him back like I meant it. Despite every reason to pull away, I can't deny how deeply I felt it too.

Thankfully, Jasmine and Olivia are working the room when I return. They're deep in conversation, doing what they do best, and oblivious to my internal turmoil. The crowd is buzzing, but nobody seems to notice that I just got my soul snatched by a six-foot-something attorney in a tailored suit. The way that man kisses should be illegal.

I still haven't figured out how I'm supposed to breathe after that kiss.

When I spot him again, he's standing across the room, straightening his suit jacket like he didn't just try to rearrange my life under the stars. He walks back over to his plus one, who's still wrapped in gold, still gorgeous, and still not me. She frowns when he leans in and whispers something in her ear. Her lips purse into a pout that would be cute if I wasn't watching it play out like a slow-burn drama.

She blinks. Then rolls her eyes. Then picks up her clutch and storms toward the exit like she's walking a runway. She doesn't cause a scene or dramatics; she just walks the type of walk that says *this isn't what I thought it was.*

David follows her outside and, for a moment, I think he's gone. I imagine them arguing, her crying, and him consoling her. That's until he returns, alone, adjusting his cufflinks like he didn't just send his plus-one packing.

He searches the room until he finds me, and his fingers graze his lips.

God help me. He's thinking about the kiss. Our kiss.

So am I.

He cuts across the ballroom like he's on a mission. His eyes are locked on mine, and he doesn't bother to hide the heat behind his gaze.

"I'd like to do what I should've done the moment I saw you tonight," he says, stopping right in front of me. His voice is low, firm, and threaded with something that makes my stomach flutter. He extends a hand. "Would you do me the honor of a dance?"

I lift an eyebrow. "What happened to your plus one?"

His jaw ticks, but his voice stays steady. "I told her I wanted to spend the rest of the night with you." He shrugs. "She went home."

Caught off guard, my lips part. "Oh."

He steps a little closer with his hand still outstretched. "So... can I have this dance?"

I glance at his hand, then up at his eyes. My heart is damn near doing backflips in my chest.

"In that case," I say, sliding my hand into his, "yes."

He leads me to the dance floor, his hand warm and steady on the small of my back as the music shifts into something soft, slow, and sensual. His other hand finds mine, and our fingers lace like they've done it a hundred times before.

We sway in sync, and for a moment, the rest of the room fades into a blur of chandeliers and string instruments. It's just us. Only us.

"So..." he starts, his voice low like it's just for me. "About earlier."

I lift an eyebrow but say nothing, letting him talk.

"She's not my girlfriend."

He watches closely, like he's measuring how much truth I'm ready to handle.

"She's someone from my past. College... law school," he says after a pause. "We were engaged once."

That hits harder than I expect, but I keep my face unreadable. "Oh," I say lightly, but I can feel my fingers tense in his.

"Yeah." He lets out a slow breath, like this is the confession he's been waiting to tell. "Her name is Danielle, and I thought we had our forever lined up for marriage, kids, the whole plan. But she had a different one."

"She left?" I ask, softer now.

He nods. "Disappeared three years ago. No goodbye. Just a note and silence. She called me a week or so ago and needed help... a place to stay for a week. That's why she's around now."

"Why did she leave you?"

"Said that she was scared of the life we were building. She was in law school too, and she was afraid of being a lawyer, of being tied to something she wasn't sure she could live up to."

"That couldn't have been easy on her."

He shrugs dismissively. "It wasn't easy on me either."

I glance up at him. "And now she's back?"

He exhales slowly. "Yeah. She needed a place to stay before her new art internship starts in New York. She's at my house for now. Just a few weeks."

I stiffen. "She's *staying* with you?"

"It's temporary. And one hundred percent innocent. But if you're not okay with it, I'll put her in a hotel. No hesitation."

I shake my head. "You don't have to change your plans for me. We're not—"

He leans in and kisses me like he's silencing every doubt with his mouth. His reassurance is deep, certain, and breath-stealing.

When he finally pulls back, his voice is low. "We *are* everything."

I blink, dazed and a little undone. "Okay... message received." Then I clear my throat and murmur, "So, about that picture on your shelf... the one that was face down..."

A hint of shame enters his eyes as he nods. "That was us. I just... never got around to putting it away. Never really faced it. Until now."

I bite my lip, then chuckle bitterly. "That's wild. She left you because she was afraid of the dream. Mine left me because he didn't believe in it."

David frowns. "What man would be stupid enough to leave you?"

"My ex. I told him I wanted to leave my finance job to open Dreamy Weddings. He told me I was being reckless. Called it trinkets and lace. Said I was throwing away everything I built."

"He sounds like an idiot," David mutters.

I smile. "In the end, I found out he was an idiot, but at one time, I thought we would be together forever. Forever walked out the door the minute I bet on myself."

He looks at me like I'm the prize. "You bet on yourself... and built something brilliant. You won if you ask me."

Our steps slow with the music.

"His loss, my gain," he says, leaning closer. "I'm looking at someone who makes the future feel like a possibility again."

My breath catches. I glance down at our hands and then back up at him.

"Only a possibility?" I tease.

He smirks, that same smooth grin that's been threatening my good sense all night. "Let me show you what happens when you let a lawyer build a case. I'm pretty convincing."

"Oh, you don't have to explain that to me, Counselor?"

He chuckles. "Say that again."

"You don't have to explain—"

"No, just the last part."

"Counselor?"

"Yeah, I like it when you call me Counselor." He laughs. "Isn't it ironic?"

"What is?"

"You were open about your dream with your ex and got left. Danielle hid hers... and left me."

"Damn," I say, blinking. "We were doomed either way."

We both laugh. It's that kind of laugh that pours out of your soul into someone else's. It could be relief or feeling connected to someone going through the same thing.

"But hey," he says, guiding me through a graceful spin, "at least now we know what it feels like to have someone that's not honest with us. We know that building trust and keeping it is important. If we mess this up, it won't be because we didn't speak up about what we're feeling."

"So, what exactly is this your speaking of?" I ask with a raised brow.

He pulls me back into his arms, his hand resting at my waist as his gaze locks with mine. He's serious, unblinking, and way too deep for me to escape.

"This," he assures, "is something I'm not letting go of."

We dance wrapped in the truth, wrapped in the possibility... Wrapped in *us*.

Chapter Twelve

David

Not Yours Anymore

The scent of bacon, cinnamon, and eggs hits me first. I rub a hand over my beard as I descend the stairs. I know what this is. Danielle's cooking *my* comfort breakfast. Just like old times. Except this isn't old times. This isn't us.

When I step into the kitchen, she's standing at the stove, barefoot, wearing one of my T-shirts and a pair of bootie shorts like she still belongs here. Like last night didn't just make everything between us clearer than ever.

She turns with a bright smile that used to have me ready to put on that Jamie Foxx Wedding Song and call a priest. Now, it barely moves the needle. "Good morning," she says, holding up a plate. "I made some of your favorites. I've got cheese eggs, cinnamon toast, and a couple slices of applewood bacon. You always liked it crispy."

I nod slowly, careful with my words. "You didn't have to cook."

"But I *wanted* to," she replies, gliding over and placing the plate on the counter. Her voice is light, but I see the intention behind her eyes. It's flirty, hopeful, and a play she's run before.

Danielle's smile falls and her brows knit as she places the plate on the counter. "I'm not pretending," she says quietly. "I'm trying. Isn't that what you wanted? For me to be here? To show up for once?"

I shake my head slowly. "No, Danielle. I wanted honesty. I wanted effort when it *mattered*. Not years later, when you've got one foot out the door again."

Her lips part like she's about to argue, but nothing comes out. Instead, she crosses her arms, defensive. "So, what? I'm just supposed to fade into the background while you chase after someone new?"

"This isn't about someone new. This is about *us*," I say. "We're not in love, and there hasn't been anything between us for a very long time."

She blinks, hurt spreading across her face before she looks away. "Then, why did you let me stay?"

I sigh. "Because I still care about you. I used to think that if I ever got you back, I'd show you how much I loved you and make you want to stay. But I don't want that anymore. I don't care like that anymore. Not in the way that matters between a man and a woman."

The loud silence after that statement causes me to break it. "You should eat before you go. Hotel check-in's at noon."

"Hotel check in?"

"Yeah, I'm taking you back to Evergreen today," I say firmly. "I'll cover your hotel room for the week until your internship starts. But you need to be in your own space—not mine."

She freezes. "Wait... what? Why have you changed your mind so suddenly?"

"Because it's time," I say. "Because I need clarity. And keeping you here doesn't offer me that. It'll only lead to confusion."

Her eyes narrow. "Did I do something wrong?"

"No." I shake my head. "You didn't do anything wrong. But this." I wave my hand back and forth between us. "Us under one roof again was a mistake."

"Is it the woman from last night?" she snaps.

I pause, and then nod. "Yes... and no. She didn't ask me to do anything. She didn't even know you were staying with me until last night. But after last night, I know what I want, and I don't want *this*. I don't want to blur lines."

Danielle shakes her head. "I have known you for years, and you're kicking me out because of her. Because you don't trust yourself around me."

I raise an eyebrow. "That's not it."

She steps closer, challenging me. "David, I know you. You're a faithful man. You've *always* been that man. You'd rather send me packing than risk getting close to me again. Because even though y'all aren't together, you're feeling her, and you don't want to cross any lines."

I take a step back. "That's a big part of it. I'm not going to lie. I am feeling her. But this conversation isn't about her. It's about us. About how we ended."

Her jaw tightens, and her eyes flash with guilt. She doesn't say a word.

"You left me, Danielle. You left a damn *note*. Not a conversation. Not a fight. A note. Like I was some college fling you were ghosting, not the man you said you wanted forever with. I spent years wondering what the hell I did wrong."

Her lips press into a thin line before she fires back. "You didn't listen to me, David. Ever. You heard what you wanted to hear and made up the rest. It was always about your plan, your path, your goals. I was just supposed to fall in line."

"That's not true—"

"It *is* true," she snaps. "Every time I said I needed space or that law school wasn't feeding my spirit, you told me to push through. That it would be worth it. That *we* would be worth it. But the deeper I went into your dream, the more I lost myself in it."

I rub my hand down my face. "You know what. Maybe you're right. Maybe I did push you too hard in a direction you didn't want to go. But you could've told me that, Danielle. How was I supposed to know you didn't want what you said you wanted? You could've said something instead of disappearing like a damn ghost."

"I did tell you!" Her voice cracks. "Over and over. You just didn't *hear* me."

"You don't get to rewrite this like I forced you into something. We were building something together."

She laughs bitterly, eyes shining now. "That's why I left you for Ray all those years ago," she says suddenly. Her voice is filled with venom. "He was more in tune with my feelings. He didn't talk *at* me. He saw me."

The name slams into me like a brick wall. I stare at her, and I can feel the disbelief pulsing in my temples.

"Ray?" I repeat. My voice is quieter and darker now. "*Victor Ray Dawson?* From high school?"

She flinches, just enough for me to know I've hit the mark. And then she goes quiet.

My chest constricts as the silence gets louder.

"You cheated on me with *Ray*?" I growl. "The same Ray who sat next to you in Mr. Carter's art class, who used to come around and dap me up like we were cool?"

"It wasn't like that," she says quickly, lifting her chin like she still has a leg to stand on.

"No?" I take a step forward, eyes locked on hers. "Then what *was* it like, Danielle? Because you left me with a letter and walked into the arms of a man who pretended to be my friend."

"It was one night," she blurts out, eyes glistening. "I was drunk, confused—"

"*And* you were supposed to be *with me!*" I cut her off, voice louder than I intend. I take a breath, stepping back again before I say something I can't take back. "You want to talk about not being seen? How could I see you when I didn't even know who you were?"

"Dav—"

"No, Danielle! You erased us. I spent three years thinking I messed up, thinking I was the reason you ran. But it was Ray?"

She looks away, shame finally catching up to her expression. "I didn't mean for it to happen like that."

"No," I say, chest tight, voice low. "But you let it."

We stand there in silence, years of unresolved history finally starting to make sense.

"You know what?" I say finally. "Why don't you call Ray and see if he can help you with a room at Evergreen Hotel because you're going to need it."

Her eyes snap back to mine. "I don't need shit. I have my own money."

I nod. "Then why'd you call *me*? Why are you here?"

Her jaw clenches again, but this time, the tears start to fall. "I called you because I *wanted* you, not needed you."

I shake my head slowly. "I guess that was another lie too. Maybe you missed your calling. You should have been an actor." I chuckle maniacally.

She tries to reach for me, to hug me, to salvage something—anything—between us, but I step back.

"You should go," I say flatly. "For real this time."

I watch as she goes to the guest bedroom to gather her things, shoving clothes into her bag with trembling hands.

This time, I feel every ounce of the betrayal. I feel the despair of being left. And the closure of finally letting go. This time, at least, I get to see her walk out.

Danielle walks to the door and stops with her overnight bag slung over one shoulder and a smaller duffel clutched tight in her other hand. I never saw bag lady in her cards, but she has chosen a life of a traveler, leaving baggage wherever she goes.

She's dressed simply in jeans, a faded hoodie, and her hair tied up in the same rushed bun she used to wear on finals week when she barely had time to sleep. But there's no trace of that determined fire in her eyes now.

Now, they're glassy with tears she doesn't want to cry in front of me.

"David—please," she says, stepping forward with one last hope.

I stop her gently, fingers closing around her arm, not harsh, but firm enough to draw the line. "I ordered you an Uber. You should go..."

Her face crumples for a moment before she nods, pressing her lips together like she's holding everything in. She turns, pulling the door open and stepping onto the porch with goodbye emanating from her spirit. "Okay, I'll leave," she says with bite in her tone.

The door clicks shut behind her, and I know this is the last time I will see her. I stand there for a while, just staring at the space where she stood. I should feel free. But all I feel is the sting of what's lost... and what never really was.

I close the door behind Danielle and press my back against it. For the first time in three years, I feel... light. I've finally unclenched something I shouldn't have been holding onto.

No more what-ifs. No more waiting around for a woman who already made her choice. She's gone. For real this time. After learning of her real betrayal, I can say I dodged a bullet.

I pull out my phone and scroll to Maya's number. My thumb hovers for half a second before I tap the call button.

She answers on the third ring.

"Maya speaking," she says, her voice a perfect blend of sass and sweetness.

"I like the way that sounds," I say, letting a smile curl in my voice.

"Oh, do you now? What do you want, Counselor?"

I chuckle. "I wanted to hear your voice. And maybe see if you'd let me take you out... somewhere that doesn't involve contracts or high-profile galas."

She's quiet and then, "What kind of somewhere are we talking?"

"Somewhere you can laugh as loud as you want. Somewhere I can watch your face when you eat something good and not feel guilty about staring."

"You tryna butter me up with food and compliments?" she teases, and I can hear the curve of her smile in every syllable.

"If it gets me a date, I'll throw in dessert too."

"Hmm. You offering cake or kisses?"

"Depends," I murmur, my voice lowering. "You want something sweet... or something that melts on contact?"

Her breath catches, just for a second, before she exhales slowly. "Well, Counselor, I see that we're skipping pleasantries now."

"I've been patient, Firecracker. Real patient. But I'm done waiting around. I want time with you alone. I want it to be uninterrupted, undeniable, and irresistible."

"That sounds... intense," she replies, but her voice has lost its playful edge. Now it's laced with anticipation.

The same thing I've been feeling since the first time she looked me in the eye and dared me to want her.

"Take all the time you need to think about it," I say, "but not too long. I'm clearing my schedule for you. I've got reservations on standby and plans that start with dinner and end wherever you let them."

She lets out a sweet and slow laugh that travels through the phone. "Have a good day, David."

"You too, Maya."

I hang up and stare at my phone like it still holds her voice. My pulse is drumming in my ears, and I'm buzzing beneath my skin, like she reached through the line and dragged her nails down my spine.

The moment I step into the shower, the ice-cold water brings all my senses alive. I need this freezing cold water to help keep it together.

Maya Thompson has me running hot in places I didn't know could burn. I lean into the water, hands braced on the tile, letting the chill ground me. But even then, all I see is the curve of her hips, the fire in her eyes, and the way she said my name like it belonged in her mouth.

Yeah. Danielle definitely had to go. I'm not missing my shot this time for anyone or anything.

Not with her.

Not with *us*.

Chapter Thirteen

Maya

Oh, I Think I Like Him

The bell over the door chimes just as I finish straightening the display table near the front. Before I can even look up, I hear my mama's voice spreading through the boutique like hot butter on a biscuit.

"Ohhh, baby! Look at this place! You better not be working yourself to death in here, Maya Simone Thompson!"

"Mama..." I groan as I turn, but the smile already blooming on my face gives me away. "What are y'all doing here?"

My dad trails in behind her, sunglasses still on like he's part of somebody's security detail. Leonard Thompson, the smoothest man I know, always walks like he owns the world even if he just walked out of Home

Depot. He gives me a wide grin and a hug that makes everything feel right.

"We came to see our baby girl and her fancy boutique," he says, taking his sunglasses off and glancing around. "Every time I come to visit, all I can say is this place is somethin' else, Maya. You girls outdid yourselves."

Mama, aka Carol "The Hurricane" Thompson, already has her phone out, taking pictures and narrating to nobody. "My baby was on the news, y'all! On the local news! In that plum-colored dress lookin' like she own the whole state of Georgia! I've been telling everyone at the church, at the salon, even the mailman about you being invited to a ball by the governor. They all know if somebody getting married, they better come to Dreamy Weddings!"

I laugh, pulling her into a hug. "Mama, please don't tell the mailman my business."

"You better hush," she says, waving me off. "He needed some joy in his day."

Olivia and Jasmine step out from the back, and Mama nearly swoons. "There go my bonus daughters! Ooh, I saw y'all on the news too! All of y'all just out here snatching edges and raising property values!"

Jasmine grins. "Mrs. Carol, you are too much."

"Am not. I'm just enough," Mama says proudly, pulling them both into hugs. "Y'all are building an empire and I'm telling you right now, when Oprah finds out, I'm gonna say I been knew!"

Daddy chuckles and folds his arms, leaning against the wall. "You know she don't need a microphone. Just wind her up and let her go."

I'm in the middle of trying to redirect Mama from giving Olivia an unsolicited hair consultation when the door opens again. This time, my whole body goes on alert because it's *him*.

David strolls in like he owns every square foot of this boutique. He has a clipboard in one hand and a bouquet of flowers in the other. Wearing black slacks, tailored coat, and crisp white shirt, the man looks like a walking courtroom fantasy. His eyes lock on mine, and boom, I forget my mama, daddy, and what they were talking about.

He smiles. "I come bearing both business and pleasure."

"Is that so?" I say, walking toward him, trying to play it cool even though my insides are doing that Beyoncé-coachella-bounce.

Mama eyes him up and down before nudging Daddy. "Oooh... I know who that is. Saw him on the news too."

I sigh. "Mama, Daddy, this is David Coleman. He's a contract attorney."

David extends his hand, cool and respectful. "It's a pleasure. You must be Mr. and Mrs. Thompson? I can see the resemblance."

Daddy shakes his hand with a knowing look. "We are. And you brought flowers to a business meeting, huh?"

David grins. "Well, when the business is this beautiful..."

"Boy, don't make me pull out my good church fan!" Mama fans herself dramatically. "Maya, you didn't tell us your contract lawyer looked like he walked out of a romance novel."

"Mama..." I groan, again.

"But I like him," Daddy says. "Got that gentleman energy. And if I'm not mistaken... y'all got the look of two people that might be planning a wedding soon."

I blink. "Wha—what?"

Mama claps her hands together. "And babies! I've been praying for grandbabies for years!"

"Mama!" I gasp, shooting her a look.

"I'm just saying," she shrugs, completely unbothered.

David chuckles under his breath, clearly enjoying every second of this circus.

He steps closer, holding out a bouquet. "I came by to see you and to go over a few things, but these are for you."

"Thank you," I say, smiling as I take them.

Jasmine leaves the front counter and walks over to ask, "Where's your design book? We've got a bride asking for a Maya-original shoe."

"Give me a sec. I'll be right back," I tell David, nodding toward the back office.

172

While I'm gone, my parents escort David into the lounge area. Not even thirty minutes have passed, I can tell from their conversation with David that they're both absolutely charmed. I can hear their laughter drifting through the boutique like they're catching up with an old friend.

"I like you, young man," Daddy says, loud enough for the whole shop to hear. "For one, you've got a solid handshake. Firm, but not too tight. Like you know who you are."

Mama adds, "And that voice? Lord have mercy, it's like dark chocolate and midnight promises. Mmm. Maya is one lucky girl." She waves her hand dramatically, fanning herself with one of our brochures.

"Alright. That's enough, Carol," Daddy grumbles.

"I thought we were giving compliments," Mama says.

Meanwhile, I'm sliding my design book back on the shelf as fast as I can so that I can rejoin my parents before they say something crazier than they've already said.

Before I can make it from around the counter, Jasmine and Olivia slide up on either side of me like they're staging a well-rehearsed intervention.

"Girl," Jasmine says, crossing her arms. "If your daddy is co-signing and your mama is blushing like she's twenty, it's a wrap. David's the one."

"For real," Olivia chimes in, smirking. "Your daddy just called him 'that respectable young brother with his head on straight.' I've never heard Mr. Thompson call anyone respectable with their head on straight except Obama."

I roll my eyes, trying to keep the goofy grin off my face. "Y'all doing the most."

"And you're not doing enough," Jasmine teases, bumping her shoulder into mine. "If you don't let this man take you out, I swear I'll go out with him again myself. Clearly, I missed something the first time."

"Jas!" I hiss, swatting her playfully.

"I'm just kidding! But for real, let the man take you out."

I roll my eyes, but I can't help the smile tugging at my lips. "You're lucky I love you," I mutter.

Jasmine grins and winks. "You're welcome, sis. I just gave you the push you needed."

Olivia sips her coffee and points at me. "We'll expect a full date report. And I mean *full*."

"You two are a mess," I say, laughing as I shake my head and smooth down my dress. I take a deep breath, grab the flowers from the counter, and walk toward the lounge area to rescue David.

When I step in, Mama's mid-laugh, her hand on his arm like she's known him forever. Daddy's nodding along; his eyes are warm with amusement. The room feels lighter than it did an hour ago, and somehow, David looks like he's always belonged here with my family.

He glances up the second I walk in. His lips pull into that slow, devastating grin that always knocks me off center. "There she is," he says, standing as if I'm someone worth rising for. "Your parents were just telling me all the embarrassing stories they could remember in a thirty-minute window."

"They've got more," I warn, narrowing my eyes at Mama. "Don't encourage them."

Mama waves a hand like she's offended. "We were just bonding. He listens well."

"He does?" I ask, letting my gaze linger on him a little longer than I should in front of my parents.

Eventually, Mama and Daddy gather their things, but not without a round of extra-long hugs and lingering smiles at David. Daddy throws him a sly look on the way out. "You keep treating her right, son. We're not shy about showing up again."

David chuckles and replies, "Pop in any time, and I'll be treating her right... as long as she will have me around. And please, bring more stories, Mr. Thompson."

Daddy chuckles. "Definitely."

"And if y'all end up at that altar, we're sitting on the front row," Mama adds with a proud grin.

I hide my face behind the bouquet, shaking my head as they wave and head for the door.

"We're gonna give y'all some space," Mama says, brushing invisible lint off my shoulder. "But don't think this is over. We're coming back to check the progress of this romance."

"Progress report due in ninety days," Daddy says with a wink. "And I better like what I see."

They leave with waves and grins, and I walk David to the back office, still holding the flowers he brought me like they're made of gold.

The moment the door clicks shut behind us, he steps close and kisses me. It isn't rushed or needy. It's deep, slow, and so full of meaning that I feel it everywhere. Like he's been holding back, waiting for the perfect moment to kiss me this way. And this... is it.

I wonder if every time he kisses me will feel like the best kiss I ever had. If my heart will flutter. If my toes will curl.

When we finally part, I'm breathless.

I whisper, "Are the flowers and kiss your way of asking me on a date?"

His warm hand trails down my arm. Leaning in again, he brushes his lips against my jaw. "It was my way of saying I'm done waiting for what I want. But yes, Maya. Let me take you out."

I smirk. "You sure you can pull yourself away from contracts long enough for a date with me?"

"I finished three before noon and delivered them with a bow. Been working like a man possessed so that I can be available for whenever you say you want to date me."

I laugh, curling my finger into his lapel. "And what exactly possessed you, Counselor?"

His eyes darken, and the look he gives me is nothing short of lethal. "You, my Firecracker. You're the case I want to win the most."

My heart stumbles in my chest, and I shake my head, grinning despite myself. "One date. That's all you're getting for now."

He leans in, lips brushing my cheek like a promise. "One date's all I need to prove my case."

I roll my eyes, but I can't fight the warmth spreading through me. "You better come correct, Counselor."

"I'd be a damn fool not to. I have to have a good report card when your parents check in in ninety days." He grins, eyes still locked on mine.

I chuckle. "My parents are something else."

"I like them a lot." He runs a finger down my jaw. "How soon can you be ready?"

I blink, caught off guard. "Wait. You mean, we're going on a date today?"

"Yes, today." He leans in. "I've waited long enough, Maya. I'm not trying to waste another minute."

I laugh softly, playing it cool even though my heart is tripping over itself. "That's quick. I don't have time to get myself ready. I—."

"Wear something comfortable and casual. We're not going to some stuffy steakhouse. I want to see the real you."

I tilt my head, narrowing my eyes. "What makes you think you can handle the real me?"

He smirks, stepping back just enough to let his eyes travel over me. "I've always loved a good challenge."

~*~

A few hours later...

I don't know what I expected when David said he had something planned, but showing up in jeans and sneakers was not part of it. The man cleans up like a GQ cover shoot on trial days, so I thought he'd show up looking like closing arguments. But nope. Just like he said, he dressed comfortable. Today he's casual fine. His jawline still looks like it was carved with intention, and those eyes make it hard to keep my dignity.

"Don't look at me like that," he says with a smirk as he opens the car door for me.

"You said to dress casual. You didn't say you'd do blue-jeans-and-charm-casual."

He chuckles, rounds the car, and gets in like he didn't just throw off my entire outfit confidence by looking as fine as he's looking.

We pull up to a mini golf course, and I blink at the giant neon gator on the sign and the ridiculousness of what's happening.

"I thought you said you wanted to see the real me. I don't see how that'll happen at a putt-putt course," I say, stepping out of the car, clutching my purse and silently cursing my choice of wedges.

David slides out of the driver's side like he's walking a runway, cool and smug. "A little competitiveness always brings out what's inside a person. It will be fun."

I shoot him a look. "Somehow when I imagined this date, playing child-sized golf with plastic clubs didn't come to mind."

He walks around to meet me, holding a pair of bright-colored putters and grinning like this is the best idea he's had all year. "Don't worry, my Firecracker. I'll go easy on you."

I raise an eyebrow. "Easy? Sir, you might be a beast in the courtroom, but I'll still wax you in whatever this is."

"Is that so?" he says, offering me a putter with mock seriousness. "Well, let the record show, Maya Thompson just declared war."

I take the putter from him and tap it against my palm. "War with wedges on. Don't play with me."

The game starts off light. I awkwardly line up my shots, and he pretends not to be watching me like I'm the prize at the end of the course. We talk trash like we've been doing it for years, laugh too loud for the sleepy suburb surrounding us, and somewhere between hole four and hole six, I realize I'm actually... having fun. Real fun. The kind that sneaks up on you and settles in your chest.

"You let me win that one," I say, narrowing my eyes after I miraculously sink a hole-in-one.

David holds his hands up. "That was all you, Firecracker. I would never cheat at mini golf."

I give him a side-eye that could burn holes in cotton.

"Okay," he concedes, laughing. "Maybe I gave you a little breathing room. You looked like you were getting frustrated, and I didn't want to ruin the moment."

I roll my eyes, stepping up to the next hole. "Watch and learn, Counselor."

This one's a little tricky. The curve of the fake green is angled weird, and I'm squinting, trying to figure out where to aim. I hear him step closer behind me.

"Here," he says, his voice low, "let me help."

Before I can turn, I feel him step behind me, his chest brushing my back, his hands sliding over mine on the putter. His breath is warm against my ear as he leans in. The contact sends a bolt of heat straight to my core.

"You want to line it up just right," he murmurs, adjusting my grip gently. "Keep your arms relaxed."

I'm not thinking about golf anymore. Not even a little bit.

His woodsy, clean, and expensive scent wraps around me. My heart's hammering, and my hands definitely are not relaxed.

"Whatever you are doing, you need to stop," I whisper, trying to keep my voice even.

He leans even closer, his lips brushing the edge of my ear. "You're the one who declared war, but can you handle it when you're under fire?"

And then he steps back like nothing just happened.

I miss the shot completely.

I straighten, flustered. "Damn."

He chuckles. "Guess I was a distraction," he says, shamelessly smug.

"Guess I should charge you for being a bad golf coach," I shoot back.

"I pay well," he says, his eyes lingering on me a moment too long, like he's already dreaming about what comes after this date.

And I'd be lying if I said I wasn't too.

Because the way he just touched me, so patient, so in control but still tender, makes me wonder what else he's good at guiding me through.

Mini golf has officially been upgraded to my new favorite sport.

"So, this your go-to first date?" I ask, leaning against my club.

He squints at me like I'm saying something outrageous. "What makes you think I do this often?"

"Because you're charming, confident, and you give off big first-date energy."

He grins. "Well, for the record... you're the only woman I've ever brought here. And I'm regretting it."

"Why?" I ask, feigning offense.

"Because you're too competitive. I'm not sure my ego can survive this."

We finish our game with me two strokes ahead. I'm convinced he let me win.

We end the night with burgers and milkshakes at this old-school diner with red leather booths and Motown music playing low. When he reaches across the table to steal a fry and I swat his hand away, it feels like we're two people who have known each other for life.

I look at him, and he looks at me like he wants to say something important. But instead, he smiles. "Let me take you out again," he says softly.

I dip a fry in ketchup and pop it in my mouth. "You trying to get beat at bowling next time?"

He laughs, but his eyes don't leave mine. "You could wear heels, throw the ball backward, and I'd still want to be in your lane."

As I sit there laughing at his corny joke, that's when I know I'm all his.

Chapter Fourteen

David

Betrayal on Betrayal

A few weeks later, I'm sitting in my office at Coleman & Williams with a fresh cup of coffee in hand, scanning over the latest Turner Enterprises deal. My attention drifts, though. These days, it's getting harder and harder to focus when my mind keeps wandering to my Firecracker.

I've been splitting my time between Turner's multi-million dollar contracts and her, except she's getting the majority of my free time. And I don't regret it for a second.

We've been on six dates so far.

The second was bowling. She showed up in this burgundy sweatsuit and crisp white sneakers, and somehow made comfort look like a fashion statement. Her hair was up, gold hoops in, and lip gloss poppin'. She swore she hadn't bowled in years but still managed to beat me in the first game. I came back with a vengeance in the second, but it didn't matter. The way she danced every time she got a strike had me ready to give her the win. I wasn't just watching her bowl. I was falling for her, one strike at a time.

We went go-kart racing next. She was ruthless and took every opportunity to cut me off. I laughed so hard I almost forgot I came there to win. She wore a cropped hoodie and tight jeans, and I swear every man on that track was distracted, but she only had eyes for me.

On our fourth date, I took her to a rooftop movie night downtown. She brought a blanket, curled up next to me, and halfway through the film, her head was on my chest and my hand was in her hair. I didn't even remember the plot of the movie, but I remember the way she looked up at me and whispered, "This is perfect."

Another night, I took her to a museum. Art and wine night. She challenged me to interpret abstract paintings like I was on some HGTV special. She was hilarious, confident, and insightful. At one point, she leaned in and whispered her interpretation of a piece. It was a painting of shattered glass and tangled lines. "This one's love," she said, "messy, raw, but still holding together."

And then there was the jazz lounge, which was her favorite. She wore this off-the-shoulder black dress that left little to the imagination and everything to desire. We slow danced, and I held her like the whole damn world was watching. Didn't care. She fit against me like she was made for my arms. That night, I almost told her I was falling.

And just last week, we went to a bookstore café. She read me poetry over lattes like her voice was meant to make words feel like honey. I didn't realize two hours had passed until they started turning chairs upside down on the tables.

So yeah. Maya has made her way into my every thought, every plan, and every break in my schedule. And I'm not mad about it.

Yolexis pops her head into my office looking uneasy. "You've got a call on line two. It's Judge Waverly."

I frown. "Judge Waverly?"

She nods. "Yes, and he says it's urgent."

I pick up the phone immediately and brace myself. "Judge," I say smoothly. "To what do I owe the pleasure?"

His voice is curt, and he offers no small talk. "David, this phone call is completely off the record. It has come to my attention that your firm has potentially leaked confidential information in the Turner-Agatha case. This information was only accessible to a select few, including you."

The blood in my veins turns cold as I try to process what he is saying. "What?"

"Did you or did you not send information to an outside party? If so, this could jeopardize the entire case Turner has against the defendant and your career."

I sit up, my mind racing. "I would never do that."

There's a pause. A sigh. Then— "An exec working for Agatha is harassing the witnesses to scare them into being quiet. The reason I know this is that a couple of those engineers and contractors who gave statements have called my office complaining that they have been contacted by either Danielle or Victor Dawson, threatening to leak their confidential witness statements."

My stomach drops as everything that's happening clicks.

It's news to me that Victor is an executive for Agatha. He's not listed in any of the paperwork related to the company. That wouldn't even be an issue if Danielle wasn't married to him and hadn't been in my house alone, rummaging through my things.

The last two weeks replay like a bad movie, and suddenly, the pieces fit. Danielle said she left me for Victor, who works for the company Turner is suing over a construction mess from a year ago.

Judge Waverly keeps talking, but my brain isn't processing his words. All I can think about is the woman who's been in my house, sitting on my couch, drinking with me, laughing like we're still those broke college kids playing Monopoly on the floor.

The woman who I thought wanted closure played me.

The thought slams into me like a MAC truck, shattering whatever nostalgia that clouded my judgement enough to let her come and stay with me. I've been trying to make sense of why she came back so suddenly. Why now? Why like this?

None of the answers she gave made sense. Then again, most people who are homeless don't have stories that make sense. Something crazy happens that sends you on a downward spiral, and the next thing you know, you're out in the cold in need of help.

So, I didn't judge.

But she said she had money on the day I put her out, which is just more proof that she wasn't here to reconnect. She was here to ruin me.

"Okay, Judge, I will have to find out what happened and get back to you later."

Judge Waverly doesn't let me off that easily.

"No, Counselor. You'll get back to me *within twenty-four hours*—with answers. If I don't have a credible explanation by then, I'll be forced to report this to the State Bar and remove your firm from the Turner case."

The words hit harder than anything Danielle's ever done to me. Turner is our biggest client. If we lose this case—or worse, if they think we compromised we'll lose the entire account. And possibly our entire reputation.

"You understand me, Counselor?"

I stand, jaw clenched, adrenaline spiking through my system. "Yes, Your Honor. I'll handle it."

There's a beat of silence before he speaks again, his voice slightly lower.

"You've always had integrity, David. Don't let me find out otherwise."

The line clicks dead.

I grip the phone until my knuckles ache. All the feelings I've been burying about Danielle—the confusion, the betrayal, the ache of what we used to be—burn away.

Now, it's war.

I'm not letting a ghost from my past destroy my present or sabotage my future.

She picked the wrong man to play with.

After a long day of plotting, strategizing, and making my position airtight with the judge, I leave the office knowing exactly what needs to be done.

I pull into Evergreen Hotel, walk straight into the lounge, and spot her at the bar, just like she said she'd be when I texted her earlier.

Danielle's sipping red wine, legs crossed, acting like she's got the world by the throat. Her smirk rises when she sees me. "Rough day, boo?"

I don't return the greeting. I don't sit. Just stand there, staring, the heat rising in my chest as realization of how low she has gone sinks in.

"How long?"

Her smirk twitches. "How long what?"

I take a step closer. "How long have you been working against me? Was it from the moment you texted me for help? Or did you wait until after we poured up that cheap E&J and played Monopoly like we were still us?"

She blinks, slow and deliberate, then shrugs with that same smug air I used to mistake for charm. "No. It was after you sent me home from the ball in an Uber. Like I didn't matter. Yep, that did it."

I shake my head, jaw tightening. "You played the victim to get into my house. To get in my head. All while running back to Victor Dawson with information about the Agatha case."

I let his name sit between us like poison.

"My husband," she finishes with a tilt of her chin. Finally, she sets her glass down with a quiet clink. "I was hoping you wouldn't catch on so fast. Would've been nice to... *reconnect*... one last time." She uses air quotes with the word 'reconnect.'

I let out a bitter laugh. "You wanted to sleep with me and sabotage me in the same week?"

Another shrug. "Two birds. One stupid man." She lets the words land, then leans back with a mocking smile. "I saw how you looked at her. Maya. You think she's different. You think you won't lose her too. But you will. Because you don't know how to love without control. And women like her don't do control."

189

I contemplate arguing with her but decide against it. "That's for me to figure out. You've got bigger problems."

She thinks she knows me. Thinks I'm still the same fool who begged her to stay. But what she doesn't know is that I've changed.

I don't need to control the right woman. I just need her to choose me back.

Unfortunately for Danielle, I'll never choose her again.

I turn back one last time. "You know what your real problem is, Danielle? You underestimated the wrong one. I might be too trusting... but I'm not stupid. Never that."

She opens her mouth to speak, but I'm already walking out.

This time, I'm the one who disappears.

And right as I step out into the hotel lobby, two plainclothes officers step past me.

They know exactly who they're here for.

Danielle King-Dawson is under arrest for theft of protected case documents and obstruction of justice.

As I keep walking, I don't feel a damn thing about her getting arrested.

I slide into the driver's seat, shut the door, and sit for a second in silence. This silence isn't hollow, aching silence Danielle left behind three years ago. It's a new kind that's clean and peaceful.

I press the ignition, then tap my phone screen and hit Jacob Turner's name. He answers before the second ring.

"Coleman."

"Mr. Turner." My voice is calm, matching my mood. "Wanted to give you a direct update. We're still good. The leak's been contained, and the person responsible is being handled by law enforcement as we speak."

There's a pause on the line, then a slow exhale. "Was it someone inside?"

"Someone with access, yes. But not someone currently affiliated with the firm or Turner Enterprises. I've already filed a motion to seal witness records and will be submitting a letter to the judge by close of business tomorrow to reaffirm the integrity of our chain of custody."

"So, you're saying we're still winning?"

I glance up at the rearview mirror, watching the blue and red lights flash through the hotel lobby windows. "I'm saying we never stopped winning."

Turner lets out a satisfied laugh of a man who sees his millions protected. "You know, when I hired you, my board said you were a little too young, too polished, too calm. I told them that's exactly why I picked you. Because calm men don't flinch when the floor shakes."

"The floor didn't shake, sir," I say, my voice flat. "It cracked. And I reinforced the damn foundation."

191

He laughs again. "Well, carry on, Coleman. Dinner's on me when we win."

"Looking forward to it."

I end the call, lean my head back, and finally let the breath I didn't know I was holding escape.

Chapter Fifteen

Maya

Control Me

I take a deep sigh of relief.

Bridezilla picked up her entire order today, and we are done with her for good, hopefully. Now, I'm working diligently on a unique shoe design for Tess, something glam but still her. Humming along to the slow R&B track playing low in the background, I zone in on the lines of the sole, rhinestone details, and satin finish. I'm so in my zone that I don't hear the door jingle, but when I hear the footsteps, my heart jumps.

Heading to the front, I notice it's David, wearing a black suit, crisp white shirt, and that crooked smirk that could get a woman in trouble. He closes and locks the store door behind him, like walking in here uninvited is a thing we do now.

"I saw Olivia and Jasmine leave out," he says, voice low and rich like the song playing. "What are you still doing here all alone?"

I straighten my back and fold my arms, trying not to show that I'm flustered. "We're closed, but I have a few things I'm working on for Tess."

"I know you're always busy," he says as he strolls in like he owns the place. "But you shouldn't be here alone."

"I had to stay to give Ambrosia her order."

"I know. I saw your Bridezilla leave out before I came in."

I chuckle. "Are you stalking me now?"

He shrugs like it's no big deal, all cool and confident. "It's a public place. Door was open."

"Well, it's closed now. So, I'm safe."

His smile turns cocky, like he knows exactly how unsafe I feel with him standing this close. He steps forward and closes the gap between us. "You want me to leave?"

My breath hitches. Damn him.

"I didn't say that," I mumble, eyes glued to his mouth.

His gaze drops to my lips, then back up. "Then say what you mean, Maya."

I hate how my name sounds deep and smooth in his mouth, like it belongs there.

I tilt my chin. "I mean... you came here with no appointment, no flowers, no coffee. And now you're all in my space, distracting me from work."

"Guilty," he says, his fingers grazing the side of my hand. "But you never mind when it's me doing the distracting."

"Don't flatter yourself," I shoot back, trying to sound unaffected even though my pulse is doing the most.

He smirks, the kind that makes my stomach flip. "I don't have to. You're already doing it for me."

I shake my head, but I don't step back.

His smile fades, and his jaw flexes. "I want to ask you something."

"Okay..." I say slowly, my arms folding out of reflex.

He looks me dead in the eye. "Do you think I'm controlling?"

The question knocks me off balance. "No," I reply honestly. "Why would you ask that?"

"Danielle said I tried to control her. That I pushed her into law school because I didn't want to be with someone who wasn't in my world. That I forced my dream onto her because I didn't trust her to have her own."

He looks away for a second, his jaw clenched tight.

"And now," he continues, voice hardening, "she hates me so much she stole confidential documents from my home and gave them to the opposing counsel just to ruin something I worked my ass off for."

Anger and heartbreak radiate off him like heat.

I stare at him, stunned.

"She has said some crazy things to me. Said I succeeded in life and she didn't and that it's my fault. That I controlled her so much, she never had a chance to figure out who she really was." He pauses, then meets my eyes again. "That messed with me, Maya. Because I thought I was helping. Pushing her to go for what she said she wanted. I thought it was motivation."

I blink, letting the confession settle. "David..."

"I just..." He runs a hand over the back of his neck. "I don't ever want to do that to anyone again. Especially not you. I don't want to think I'm helping when I'm really pushing you away. I want you to always feel safe with me. To know I'll never try to shape you into something you're not. I want to know your dreams so I can protect them—not pressure you."

For a moment, I can't speak. Everything he just said is the exact opposite of what I had.

"You know I had someone who didn't believe in me," I finally manage to say. "My ex, Troy, didn't think Dreamy Weddings was worth a discussion. He called it a hobby. Said I was reckless for giving up a secure career in finance to chase a dream of trinkets and lace."

David's face hardens.

"So, what you were trying to give Danielle?" I say, stepping closer. "That belief? That support? I would have *died* for that. I fought to build this place without it. So, no—you're not controlling. You just loved someone who didn't know how to love you back. Because that would have started with her being honest with herself and you."

He takes that in, breathing shallow breaths.

"Thank you for saying that," he says, stepping closer until we're almost touching.

"It's true," I whisper. "Let it all go. She didn't deserve you."

He nods slowly, then drops his gaze to my lips.

This time, he doesn't look away.

"You know what," he murmurs, his voice sending heat straight through me, "I think about kissing you every single night before I close my eyes."

I swallow hard, heart pounding in my ears. "You're not the only one," I admit, my voice barely a breath.

He steps forward until we're chest to chest. His hand finds my waist, and he leans in, brushing his mouth just over the corner of mine, like he's giving me a chance to stop him.

When our lips meet again, it's not frantic like the first time. It's deep and sure, a kiss made from relief, release, and something that feels a hell of a lot like falling in love.

I suck in a shaky breath. "David..."

"Tell me to stop," he says, hand sliding to my hip.

I don't.

I can't.

Instead, I lift my chin and whisper, "Let's go to the back."

He takes me by the hand, leading me to my office. Once inside, he's back standing in front of me, all heat and want and temptation. It's apparent I'm prepared to fold like laundry as my fingers twitch at my sides. All he has to do is touch me, and I'll melt.

When his hand brushes the curve of my waist, I disintegrate.

That is the control he has over me.

"What do you want from me?" I whisper. "Do you want a girlfriend, a wife...a fling—what?"

His voice drops even lower, intimate. "Everything."

I gasp, and the second I do, his lips are on mine.

It's fire. Raw, unfiltered fire traveling between us as his hands slide over my body like he's memorizing it. I grab fistfuls of his blazer, pulling him closer, needing the kiss just as much as he does. He lifts me onto the desk like it's second nature, steps between my thighs, and presses me into him like I'm his next breath.

"Tell me you want this," he murmurs against my lips, eyes searching mine.

I bite down on his bottom lip just enough to make him growl. "I want this."

The room is still. Even time knows not to interrupt this moment.

David's mouth is on mine again, but it's different this time. He's slower and hungrier. He's memorizing me with every kiss and graze of his tongue. His hands roam my body like I'm something sacred, something he's only dreamed of touching.

This kiss isn't like the ones we've shared at the end of our dates. This one can match our first kiss on the balcony. Oh, no, this kiss can top that one.

I curl my fingers into the lapels of his blazer and push it off his shoulders. He lets it fall without care, his hands already sliding down my back. One tug at the zipper of my dress and it loosens, sliding down my body inch by inch, guided by his fingers.

He groans when it pools around my heels, leaving me in a lace bra and panties. His hands grip my hips like he's trying to ground himself.

"Maya..." he whispers, as if saying my name out loud might shatter whatever control he's holding onto.

"I want you," I whisper back, breathless.

That's all it takes.

He lifts me onto the desk like I weigh nothing. My legs wrap around his waist instinctively, pulling him in, desperate to close the space between us. He kisses me hard, and I meet him with everything I've got. Weeks of stolen glances, lingering touches, and words left unsaid all pour into this kiss.

His jacket is gone, shirt unbuttoned, muscles warm under my hands. I run my fingers over his chest, feeling the tension in every breath he takes. When his lips trail down my neck, my head falls back with a soft gasp.

"I've been dreaming about this," he murmurs, kissing along the swell of my breast. "About you."

He peels my bra away slowly, his mouth replacing the lace, leaving fire in its place. I can't keep quiet as he kisses his way down to my thighs. I don't want to. I want him to hear what he's doing to me.

My hands fumble with his belt, desperate to feel more of him. He helps, guiding my hands with his own, never breaking eye contact. His pants fall just enough, and I feel his thickness.

He grips my waist, lining us up, and then—

"Oh my God," I gasp as he enters me, slow and deep, filling me completely.

He pauses, his forehead resting against mine. "You okay?"

I nod, breath hitching. "Better than okay."

He moves inside of me, making each stroke count. They are deep, like he's carving his name into my soul. His fingers clutch my thighs, his body pressing into mine over and over until I'm arching against him, nails digging into his back, whispering his name like a mantra.

"David..."

"I've got you," he says between gritted teeth. "I've got you, Firecracker."

My body tightens around him, trembling as the waves crash over me. I cry out, shattering against him. He follows with a growl, holding me tight as he spills into me, shaking with the force of it.

For a long moment, we just breathe. Wrapped in each other, heartbeats syncing, chests heaving.

When he finally pulls back to look at me, his eyes are soft. Full.

"You okay?" he asks again, brushing my hair from my face.

I nod, still catching my breath. "You?"

He grins. "You just rocked every bit of sense out of me."

I laugh, resting my head against his shoulder. "That makes two of us. I just lost all of my good sense. Since professionalism is out the window, guess we should keep the boutique stocked with mints and a blanket or two."

He chuckles, his arms tightening around me. "No complaints here. But next time, I'm taking you to a bed."

I lift my head and kiss him again, slow and sweet.

"Next time," I whisper, "you're not taking me anywhere. I'll be the one taking you."

His smile is pure sin. "Say less."

The next morning, and all mornings after, I wake up wrapped in David's arms, and I won't lie... I love it here.

Epilogue

David

One Month Later

Amiri and Tess's Wedding Day

Tess's wedding is everything Maya promised it would be. It's magical, seamless, and somehow still full of joy despite all the moving parts she and her team have had to maneuver. It's not just the flowers or the glowing bride that hold my attention all night.

It's her.

I am in complete awe of her as I watch her work.

Maya moves through the room like she owns it, greeting vendors, fluffing Tess's train, whispering last-minute cues to the DJ. That new plum-colored dress she slipped into after the ceremony clings to every curve like it was designed just for this night, and watching her command the room with poise and purpose... yeah. This is the moment.

I've carried the ring for two weeks. Waiting. Watching. Wanting.

And suddenly, I know this is the time. We have only known each other for two months, but I'm done waiting. When you know, you know.

Tess and Amiri are dancing, swaying under the soft glow of fairy lights, when Maya finally returns to our table with a satisfied smile on her lips and a well-earned glass of champagne.

"You crushed it," I say, rising to meet her. "Everything about tonight... it's perfect. You're perfect."

She raises an eyebrow, amused. "Compliment me like that again and I'll start charging you for emotional labor."

I laugh, taking her hand and guiding her a step away from the crowd. I tap my glass with a fork and clear my throat, catching the attention of Jasmine, Olivia, Will, Brielle, Tess, and even Amiri.

"I know this isn't our moment," I say, voice steady but loud enough to carry. "But sometimes, love doesn't wait for the spotlight. Sometimes... it steals it."

Maya's smile falters as realization begins to dawn, her eyes widening as I drop to one knee and pull the velvet box from inside my blazer.

Gasps ripple across the crowd.

Jasmine claps her hands over her mouth. Olivia yells, "Oh, it's happening!" and Tess grabs Amiri's arm like she might fall out right there on the dance floor.

"Maya Thompson," I begin, my voice low but sure. "From the moment you challenged my contracts, to the moment you stole my breath at the Governor's Ball... I knew."

She presses her hands to her chest, her lip trembling.

"I asked your parents for their blessing," I continue. "And mine are in full support too. I was going to wait, plan something big, but watching you tonight, running this event like it was yours, and watching you thrive, I realized I didn't want to wait another second."

I open the box. The diamond sparkles like it knows it's going home.

"I want to build everything with you. A life, a legacy, a family... all of it. So tell me, Maya. Will you marry me?"

The crowd erupts in cheers, Olivia squealing as Jasmine literally jumps up and down.

Maya's eyes are full now, brimming with tears she's not even trying to hide. She drops to her knees in front of me, throws her arms around my neck, and whispers, "Every moment with you feels like our moment."

I wrap my arms around her tightly.

"That's a yes," she breathes, then laughs into my ear. "But if you ever try to upstage my clients again, I'm giving the ring back."

"Fair enough," I murmur, slipping the ring onto her finger. "But I did ask them both if it would be okay, and they gave me the greenlight."

"You did?" she asks, looking up at Amiri and Tess who are nodding and holding hands.

"Yes," Tess says. "He did so much for us to help us get to this day, how could we say no?" She smiles at Amiri like he hung the stars and the moon.

When David stands, Amiri daps him up and says, "Thanks man. I wish you the best."

Everyone's clapping and congratulating us.

Tess clutches her bouquet to her chest like she's enjoying the moment as much as her wedding. "I knew you two would get together. You two are perfect for each other."

I pull Maya into my arms again, holding her close as the celebration ensues around us. We dance for minutes, or was it hours? For me, time slows. Everything fades into the background. The lights, the noise, the crowd are all faint and a blur.

All I see is her. All I want is her.

This time, two hearts are aligned.

And I didn't miss the moment. I seized it, created it, and fought for it.

I won the only case that ever truly mattered. Not in court. Not on paper. But the case to prove she belongs right here... in my arms.

The case for Maya Thompson's heart has been won.

From this day forward, it won't be contracts or chaos that define us. It will be love. It will be trust. It will be *Only Us.*

I hope you enjoyed Maya and David's story.

You can read more about the demanding billionaire, Jacob Turner, in the Breathless series and more about Tess's husband/best friend dilemma in Taken by the Billionaire.

Join my mailing list at www.shanigreenedowdell.com for updates on new releases!

Made in the USA
Columbia, SC
10 June 2025

59101613R00115